I0661258

Charles G. D. Roberts

Poems of Wild Life

Charles G. D. Roberts

Poems of Wild Life

ISBN/EAN: 9783744765343

Printed in Europe, USA, Canada, Australia, Japan

Cover: Foto ©Andreas Hilbeck / pixelio.de

More available books at **www.hansebooks.com**

POEMS OF WILD LIFE.
SELECTED AND EDITED
BY CHARLES G. D. ROBERTS,
M.A.

Author of " Orion and other Poems," and " In Divers Tones." Professor of English and French Literature in King's College, Windsor, Nova Scotia, Canada.

LONDON
WALTER SCOTT, 24 WARWICK LANE
TORONTO : W. J. GAGE AND CO.
1888

INDEX.

BRYANT, WILLIAM CULLEN—   PAGE

    An Indian Story 1
    The African Chief 4
    The Arctic Lover 6

CHENEY, JOHN VANCE—

    How Squire Coyote brought fire to the Cahrocs . 7
    The End of Sir Coyote 13

DUVAR, JOHN HUNTER—

    From "De Roberval"—Act II., Scene 6 . . . 16

EATON, ARTHUR WENTWORTH—

    The Death of De Soto 22

FAWCETT, EDGAR—

    Tiger to Tigress 25
    A Vengeance 26

GILDER, RICHARD WATSON—

    The Voice of the Pine 28

GUINEY, LOUISE IMOGEN—   PAGE
    The Wild Ride 30

HAMILTON, IAN—
    The Ballad of Hadji (Indian Boar Hunt) . . 31

HORNE, RICHARD HENGIST—
    Hajarlis 41
    The Fair of Almachara 44
    From "Arctic Heroes" 50

DE KAY, CHARLES—
    The Maid of the Beni Yezid 54

LANIER, SIDNEY—
    The Revenge of Hamish 57

MACHAR, AGNES MAUD—
    The Passing of Clote Scarp 63

MACINTYRE, DUNCAN BAN—
    Bendourain, the Otter Mount 66

MACKAY, ROBERT—
    The Song of Winter 74

MAIR, CHARLES—
    From "Tecumseh"—Act II., Scene 1. Act V., Scene 2 78

MILLER, JOAQUIN—
    With Walker in Nicaragua 84
    Kit Carson's Ride 106
    Dead in the Sierras 111
    After the Boar Hunt 112
    From "Arizonian" 113
    From "The Last Taschastas" 120

O'REILLY, JOHN BOYLE—   PAGE

Golu 124
The Dukite Snake 126
The Dog Guard 131
The Amber Whale 137
A Savage 149

POCOCK, H. REGINALD A.—
The Ranchman's Bridal 150

PRINGLE, THOMAS—
Afar in the Desert 151

ROBERTS, CHARLES GEORGE DOUGLAS—
"The Quelling of the Moose" 154
How the Mohawks set out for Medoctec . . 156

SANGSTER, CHARLES—
The Snows 159

SHARP, WILLIAM—
The Stock-Driver's Ride 161
The Isle of Love 163
The Corroboree 188

STEDMAN, EDMUND CLARENCE—
Christophe 189

STODDARD, RICHARD HENRY—
The Sledge at the Gate 191
Yes, we are merry Cossacks 192
He rode from the Khora Tukhan 192
Forgive me, mother dear 193

viii INDEX.

TEGNÉR, ESAIAS— PAGE
From "Fridthjof's Saga"—
Fridthjof at Sea 194
Balder's Pyre 201
The Election to the Kingdom . . 205

THOMPSON, MAURICE—
The Death of the White Heron 208
The Fawn 212

WARNER, HORACE E.—
The Flight of the Red Horse 214

WHITMAN, WALT—
Song of the Redwood Tree 221
From far Dakotah's Shore . . , . 226

NOTES 231

INTRODUCTION.

N making my selections for this volume of wild-life poems, I have taken no thought for complete- ness. The scope of such a collection might naturally be regarded as embracing the field of earlier folk-song—the verse produced by peoples just emerging from barbarism ; but for immediate- ness of interest I have concerned myself in the main with that characteristically modern verse which is kindled where the outposts of an elaborate and highly self-conscious civilisation come in contact with crude humanity and primi- tive nature. The element of self-consciousness, I think, is an essential one to this species of verse, which delights us largely as affording a measure of escape from the artificial to the natural. · Such escape is not to be achieved unless the gulf between be bridged for us. This the poet effects by

depicting wild existence and untrammelled action in the light of a continual consciousness of the difference between such existence and our own. To have any articulate message of enticement for our imaginations, the life of the wilds must be brought into relation with what we have experienced or conceived. We must be able to imagine ourselves as thrown into like situations, as confronted with like emergencies. The action or the situation comes home to us through the personality of such a one as ourselves, who is thoroughly in touch with the life he is describing, yet consciously belongs to a wider sphere. By such medium the most remote phases of human existence, the most unfamiliar aspects of the natural world, are drawn easily within range of our sympathies.

Such wild-life verse as this is essentially a product of later days. The first waves of civilisation which, within the last century or two, washed into the wilderness of the east and west, consisted mainly of the pioneer element. These pioneers were men wholly engrossed in action. After them came some who fled from the weariness of the artificial and the conventional, and who were able to give imaginative expression to their delight in the change. By a natural reaction, it is to the most highly-developed society that such writings as they produced make strongest appeal, restoring confidence in the reality of the universal and original impulses, and re-emphasising the distinction between the essentials and the accessories of life. In the struggling civilisations which give birth to them, however, these writings are apt to be regarded with distaste. It is to the voice from the drawing-room, rather, that the wilderness hearkens, so the better to keep itself reminded of the ideal toward which it works.

From American writers, taking all in all, comes our most abundant and distinctive wild-life verse —and it is from English readers that this verse wins its most cordial appreciation. The prince of all wild-life poets is the "Poet of the Sierras," Joaquin Miller, an American of the Americans, to whom the Old World hearkens with delight, but whom the New World eyes askance. English critics place Miller in the front rank of American singers. American critics, on the other hand, though granting him, not over willingly, a measure of genius, will allow him no such standing as an equality with Longfellow or with Lowell. The

case illustrates what I have suggested in a pre-
ceding paragraph. Our civilisation on this side
the Atlantic has not quite outgrown the remembrance of its early struggles. The riper portions
of America and Canada have attained a degree of
culture not distinguishable, at its best, from that
of the Old World; but we are not yet satisfied
that the Old World appreciates this fact. We are
so few generations from the pioneer that his hard
experiences have not yet, to our eyes, put on the
enchanting purples of remoteness. We have a
tendency to accentuate our regard for culture, for
smoothness, for conventionality; and we sometimes betray a nervous apprehension lest writings
descriptive of the life on our frontiers should be
mistaken as descriptive of our own life. Miller's
work, almost in its very defects, answered to an
Old World need. There, consequently, it found
fitting recognition. To New World life it had less
to give, outside of its purely poetic qualities; and
its faults were just such as the New World civilisation had been at such pains to outgrow. Moreover, and worst of all, this work was taken by
the Old World as a typical New World product, in which capacity, of course, it had to be

emphatically repudiated. In very truth, the bizarre experiences which inspire such verse as Miller's, such prose as that of Bret Harte, are as foreign to the typical American as to the typical Englishman,—and much less to the former's liking.

The genius of Miller is peculiarly fitted to bring this kind of verse to perfection. By nature, by temperament, he belongs to a self-conscious and long-established society. He is continually analysing himself in others. He is always holding himself sufficiently apart from his surroundings to be able to analyse their savour to the full. At the same time, his intense human sympathy keeps him in touch with the subject of his observation ; and a childhood spent in his wild Oregon home, the associations of his youth and early manhood among the turbulent pioneers and miners of the Pacific coast, have so indelibly impressed his genius, that the master-passions alone, and those social problems only that are of universal import, concern him when his singing robes are on. There is thus a primitive sincerity in his expression, and in his situations a perennial interest. His passion is manly, fervent, wholesome ; and the frankness of it particularly refreshing in these indifferent days. He is a lover of sonorous rhythms, and betrays here and there in his lines the enthralling cadences of Swinburne. But in spite of such surface resemblances, he is fundamentally as original as fresh inspiration, novel material, and a strongly individualised genius might be expected to make him. My excuse for singling out the work of Joaquin Miller for special comment is the fact that such poems as "With Walker in Nicaragua," "Kit Carson's Ride," "Arizonian," and many others for which I would fain have found space, appear to me the most characteristic work of their kind. They are just such poems as our dilettante-ridden society is in need of.

The active romantic element present in all this wild-life verse,—pre-eminently in the verse of Joaquin Miller,—makes it of special significance to us in these days, when poetry has become too much a matter of *technique*, too little a matter of inspiration. The saving grace we moderns are apt to lack is that of a frank enthusiasm. We are for ever lauding the virtue of restraint, and expounding the profound significance of repose. There has been so much talk of the repose of

conscious strength, that one is apt to forget about
the repose of conscious weakness.

"Calm's not life's crown, though calm is well."

He is but a little poet who dares not show himself moved. The great ones, both of earlier and
later days, have been ready enough to throw off
their repose when they would exert their utmost
strength. A familiarity with the work of our wild-
life singers may bring question upon the modern
poetic dogma of justification by restraint. It may
also assist, not inappreciably, in that renascence of
a true romantic spirit, toward which some of our
best spirits look for the rejuvenation of our song.
Out of what is called Romanticism has arisen the
most stimulative poetry, the poetry for poets, the
poetry of Shakespeare and the Elizabethans, of
Chatterton, of Coleridge, of Keats. And the
quality of stimulation is that which the true poet
should desire above all else, even if at the expense
of the conservation of his verse. The torch that
conveys the light to a score of waiting beacons,
though its flame smoulder thereafter, is not less
worthy than the brightest and most enduring of
those signal-fires of whose incandescence it was

the parent. The elements of romance lie thick in the life about us, but the tendency is to ignore them lest we should seem to wear our heart on our sleeve. An example of greater frankness and sincerity may not be lost upon us.

Let me not be misunderstood, however, as joining in the present too common cry of critics, that our poetry is in process of decadence. This age has still singing for it rather more than its share of master-poets, to whom it were the height of folly to imagine that my talk of "the minds of the day," and "dilettantism," in any degree applied. My words are of the young men from among whom must come the masters of the future generation. Among the young poets, with all their admirable dexterity, there is a too general lack of romance, of broad human impulse, of candid delight in life. To them such verse as that of Miller and his fellows contains a message of power.

The reader will doubtless miss from this collection many poems which he would have considered appropriate to it. For some of these omissions it is quite possible either my judgment or my knowledge may be at fault. In certain cases, again, I have had no choice. There are poems by Bayard

Taylor, Bret Harte, and others, which I greatly wished to include ; but the veto of the single firm of publishers concerned intervened. Many fine poems, moreover, I have thought well to omit as being already household words. There is a large section of wild-life verse which lies open to the charge of having been written rather from reading than from experience. This is but scantily represented. The literature of America, about a generation back, was blossoming most exuberantly with poems on the American Indian. As a rule this work was not effective ; and the little of it that was genuinely fine and strong has become so hackneyed as to lie without my purpose. The field of Australian song, whence I thought to have gathered for my collection many of its choicest and most distinctive ornaments, has been pre-empted by Mr. Sladen in his *Australian Ballads and Rhymes*, a late predecessor of the present volume in the series to which both belong. I am indebted to Mr. Sladen, however, for having left to me the picturesque and virile work of Mr. John Boyle O'Reilly. To the living authors represented in this collection I owe grateful acknowledgment for the courteous and liberal

b

assistance which they have rendered me. To certain other poets, not herein represented, I take the opportunity of expressing my thanks for a goodwill which is none the less appreciated because the firm of publishers already alluded to refused to second it. I have also gratefully to record my obligations to the following publishers, who were most generous in granting me permission to select from their copyright works :—

Messrs. Charles Scribner & Sons, D. Appleton & Co., Ticknor & Co., S. C. Griggs & Co.

CHARLES G. D. ROBERTS.

King's College, Windsor, Nova Scotia.

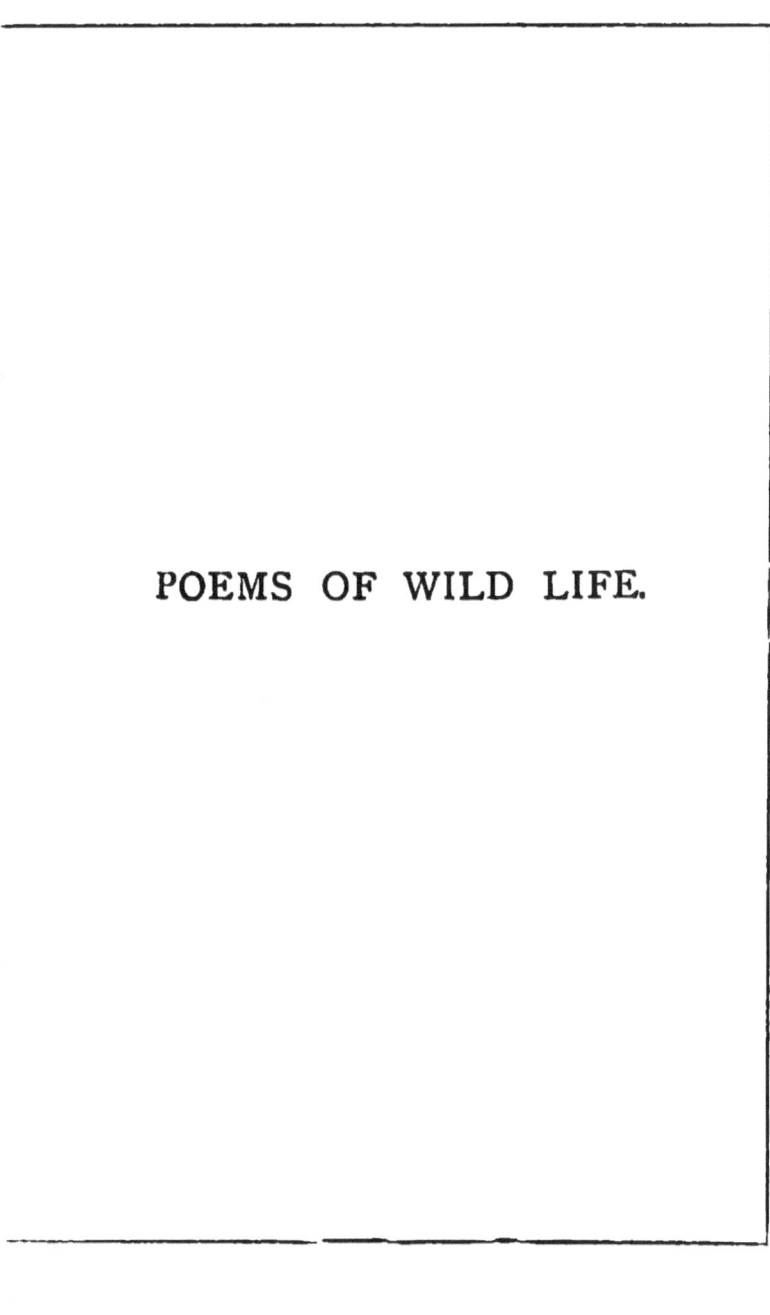

POEMS OF WILD LIFE.

Poems of Wild Life.

AN INDIAN STORY.

" I KNOW where the timid fawn abides
    In the depths of the shaded dell,
Where the leaves are broad and the thicket hides,
With its many stems and its tangled sides,
    From the eye of the hunter well.

" I know where the young May violet grows,
    In its lone and lowly nook,
On the mossy bank, where the larch-tree throws
Its broad dark bough, in solemn repose,
    Far over the silent brook.

" And that timid fawn starts not with fear
    When I steal to her secret bower ;
And that young May violet to me is dear,
And I visit the silent streamlet near,
    To look on the lovely flower."

Thus Maquon sings as he lightly walks
    To the hunting-ground on the hills ;
'Tis a song of his maid of the woods and rocks,
With her bright black eyes and long black locks,
    ᵞAnd voice like the music of rills.

He goes to the chase—but evil eyes
　Are at watch in the thicker shades ;
For she was lovely that smiled on his sighs,
And he bore, from a hundred lovers, his prize,
　The flower of the forest maids.

The boughs in the morning wind are stirred,
　And the woods their song renew,
With the early carol of many a bird,
And the quickened tune of the streamlet heard
　Where the hazels trickle with dew.

And Maquon has promised his dark-haired maid,
　Ere eve shall redden the sky,
A good red deer from the forest shade,
That bounds with the herd through grove and glade,
　At her cabin-door shall lie.

The hollow woods, in the setting sun,
　Ring shrill with the fire-bird's lay ;
And Maquon's sylvan labours are done,
And his shafts are spent, but the spoil they won
　He bears on his homeward way.

He stops near his bower—his eye perceives
　Strange traces along the ground—
At once to the earth his burden he heaves ;
He breaks through the veil of boughs and leaves ;
　And gains its door with a bound.

But the vines are torn on its walls that leant,
　And all from the young shrubs there
By struggling hands have the leaves been rent,
And there hangs on the sassafras, broken and bent,
　One tress of the well-known hair.

But where is she who, at this calm hour,
  Ever watched his coming to see ?
She is not at the door, nor yet in the bower ;
He calls—but he only hears on the flower
  The hum of the laden bee.

It is not a time for idle grief,
  Nor a time for tears to flow ;
The horror that freezes his limbs is brief—
He grasps his war-axe and bow, and a sheaf
  Of darts made sharp for the foe.

And he looks for the print of the ruffian's feet
  Where he bore the maiden away ;
And he darts on the fatal path more fleet
Than the blast that hurries the vapour and sleet
  O'er the wild November day.

'Twas early summer when Maquon's bride
  Was stolen away from his door ;
But at length the maples in crimson are dyed,
And the grape is black on the cabin-side—
  And she smiles at his hearth once more.

But far in the pine-grove, dark and cold,
  Where the yellow leaf falls not,
Nor the autumn shines in scarlet and gold,
There lies a hillock of fresh dark mould,
  In the deepest gloom of the spot.

And the Indian girls, that pass that way,
  Point out the ravisher's grave ;
" And how soon to the bower she loved," they say,
" Returned the maid that was borne away
  From Maquon the fond and the brave."

W. C. Bryant.

THE AFRICAN CHIEF.

CHAINED in the market-place he stood,
  A man of giant frame,
Amid the gathering multitude
  That shrank to hear his name—
All stern of look and strong of limb,
  His dark eye on the ground :-
And silently they gazed on him,
  As on a lion bound.

Vainly, but well, that chief had fought,
  He was a captive now,
Yet pride, that fortune humbles not,
  Was written on his brow.
The scars his dark broad bosom wore
  Showed warrior true and brave ;
A prince among his tribe before,
  He could not be a slave.

Then to his conqueror he spake :
  " My brother is a king ;
Undo this necklace from my neck,
  And take this bracelet ring,
And send me where my brother reigns,
  And I will fill thy hands
With store of ivory from the plains,
  And gold dust from the sands. "

" Not for thy ivory nor thy gold
  Will I unbind thy chain ;
That bloody hand shall never hold
  The battle-spear again.

A price that nation never gave
  Shall yet be paid for thee ;
For thou shalt be the Christian's slave
  In lands beyond the sea."

Then wept the warrior chief and bade
  To shred his locks away ;
And one by one, each heavy braid
  Before the victor lay.
Thick were the platted locks, and long,
  And closely hidden there
Shone many a wedge of gold among
  The dark and crisped hair.

" Look, feast thy greedy eye with gold
  Long kept for sorest need ;
Take it—thou askest sums untold—
  And say that I am freed.
Take it—my wife, the long, long day,
  Weeps by the cocoa-tree,
And my young children leave their play
  And ask in vain for me."

" I take thy gold, but I have made
  Thy fetters fast and strong,
And ween that by the cocoa-shade
  Thy wife will wait thee long."
Strong was the agony that shook
  The captive's frame to hear,
And the proud meaning of his look
  Was changed to mortal fear.

His heart was broken—crazed his brain :
  At once his eye grew wild ;
He struggled fiercely with his chain,
  Whispered, and wept, and smiled ;

Yet wore not long those fatal bands,
  And once, at shut of day,
They drew him forth upon the sands,
  The foul hyena's prey. .

W. C. Bryant.

THE ARCTIC LOVER.

GONE is the long, long winter night ;
  Look, my belovèd one !
How glorious, through his depths of light,
  Rolls the majestic sun !
The willows, waked from winter's death,
Give out a fragrance like thy breath—
  The summer is begun !

Ay, 'tis the long bright summer day :
  Hark to that mighty crash !
The loosened ice-ridge breaks away—
  The smitten waters flash ;
Seaward the glittering mountain rides,
While down its green translucent sides,
  The foamy torrents dash

See, love, my boat is moored for thee
  By ocean's weedy floor—
The petrel does not skim the sea
  More swiftly than my oar.
We'll go where, on the rocky isles,
Her eggs the screaming sea-fowl piles
  Beside the pebbly shore.

Or, bide thou where the poppy blows,
   The wind-flowers frail and fair,
While I, upon his isle of snow,
   Seek and defy the bear.
Fierce though he be and huge of frame,
This arm his savage strength shall tame,
   And drag him from his lair.

When crimson sky and flamy cloud
   Bespeak the summer o'er,
And the dead valleys wear a shroud
   Of snows that melt no more,
I'll build of ice thy winter home,
With glistening walls and glassy dome,
   And spread with skins the floor.

The white fox by thy couch shall play ;
   And, from the frozen skies,
The meteors of a mimic day
   Shall flash upon thine eyes.
And I—for such thy vow—meanwhile
Shall hear thy voice and see thy smile,
   Till that long midnight flies.

                      W. C. Bryant.

HOW SQUIRE COYOTE BROUGHT FIRE TO THE CAHROCS.*

In the beginning Chareya made fire
(That is, the Cahrocs say so),
Housed it safe with two beldams dire,
And meant to have it stay so.
But the Cahrocs declared that fire should be free,

     * The Coyoté : the Prairie wolf.

Not jealously kept under lock and key.
Crafty Squire Coyote,
—Counsellor of note, he,—
Just such a case he was meant for :
Forthwith his honour was sent for.

Squire Coyote came.   On hearing the case,
The cunningest smile passed over his face ;
Then, slyly winking,
In the midst of his thinking
He stopt, stopt short.
An emphatic snort,
And said he : "Tight spot,
'Twere vain to conceal it :
Very sorry you're in it.
But, though tight as a Gordian knot,
What are you 'bout
That you don't get out ?
It's only the work of a minute :
The way to get fire is to—*steal* it."
Squire Coyote was right—every Cahroc knew it,
But (bless them !) how were they going to do it ?
"Ah !" said Coyote,
Stroking his goatee
And taking his hat,
" Let me 'tend to that."
Then, airily bowing to left and right,
He scampered away, and was out of sight.

Fire for the Cahroc nation !
Coyote made preparation.
From the land of the Cahrocs afar to the East
—The rough, he knew every inch of the road—
Was stationed, now here, now there, a beast,
All the way to the hut where the hags abode.

The weaklings farthest off he put,
The strong ones nearest the witches' hut ;
And lastly, hard by the guarded den,
Placed one of the sinewy Cahroc men.

This done, up he trotted, and tapped,
The gentlest possible, rapped
At the old crones' smoky door.
"Beg pardon for being so bold ;
Fact is, I am numb with cold :
Pray give me a bed on your floor."
The trick succeeded ; they let him in,
And, snug at the feet of the beldams dire,
He stretched his length to the open fire.

Not long he lay, when, oh, the din,
The drubbing sudden heard outside !
Such a bumping and banging,
Such a whacking and whanging !
"Itch to your skins !" the witches cried,
And rushed from the hut to see
What the horrible noise could be.

Now, it was only the Cahroc man
Playing his part of Coyote's plan ;
But the simple old crones, you can well
    understand,
Didn't see through it,
And, before they knew it,
Coyote was off with a half-burnt brand.
Twitching and whisking it,
Switching and frisking it,
The best he knew,
Away he flew,

The Cahrocs' laughter
And the crones close after.
Over hill and dale,
Like a comet's tail,
Sweeps the borrowed brand
Toward Cahroc-land.
But the crones are fleet and strong,
And it can't be long
Before Coyote is made to feel
How wicked a thing it is to steal.
His spindling pegs
—Mere spider legs—
Nature never designed 'em
To match the big shanks behind 'me

He runs as never wolf ran ;
Every muscle and nerve,
All his wild-wood verve,
Is put to the strain ;
But, scratch it the fastest he can,
The gray hags gain,
And the race must soon be over.
Race over ? See there—who's that ?
Zounds ! What a monstrous cat !
It's the cougar sprung from his cover.
Ha, ha ! All but from the head crone s hand
His jaws have rescued the precious brand,
And he's off like shot !
" On time to a dot,"
Coughs Coyote, clearing the soot
From his throat and the specks from his eyes;
" Bravo, my gallant brute !—
And still the good fire flies ! "

Fly it had to. You wouldn't believe old bones
Could scuttle as now did the legs of the crones.

The witches were marvellous fleet and strong,
But, you see, the line of the beasts was too long :
From the cougar the brand was passed to the
　　bear,
And so on down to the fox, to the hare,
Thence on and on, till, flat in their tracks,
The crones collapsed like empty sacks.
Thus the brand was brought from the beldams' den
Safe to the homes of the Cahroc men.

And only two mishaps
'Mongst all the scampering chaps
That, each from the proper place,
Took his turn in the fire-brand chase.
The squirrel, as sudden he whirled,
Turning a corner of stumps and boulders
Burned his beautiful tail, so it curled
Clean over his back,
And scorched a brown track,
Still seen (tail also) over his shoulders.

The frog, poor thing !
His was a harder fate.
Small as smallest coal in the grate
Was the brand when he got it.
Jump and spring
He did, till he thought it
Was safe ; when, pounce, like a stone,
Fell the claws of the foremost crone.
At last
He was fast ;
No sort of use
To try to get loose
His eyeballs bulged, his little heart thumped—
'Most broke his ribs, so hard it bumped.

So frightened he was, that, down to this day,
He looks very much in the same scared way.

The frog was caught,
Was squeezed
Till he wheezed ;
But not too tight
For just a mite
Of ranine thought .
" Co-roak, chug, choke,
Granny Hag, good joke.
Well you've followed it ;
So move up your hand
And take your old brand "—
Then he swallowed it !
And before the crone could wholly recover
From the sight of such a wonder,
Slipping her fingers from under,
He plunged into a pool all over.
He had saved the brand,
But the witch's hand
Still clutched his special pride and care—
His tail, piteously wriggling there.
Henceforth—he must grin and bear it —
The tadpole alone was to wear it.

At length, when the crones had gone,
He sought an old log, and got on :
" Rather short of beauty,
But I did my duty ;
That's enough for a frog."
Then he spat on the log,
Spat the swallowed spark
Well into its bark.

Fire, fire to your heart's desire ;
Fire, fire for the world entire :
It's free as air to everybody,
White man or Cahroc, wise man or noddy.

From the beldams' den,
A gift to all men,
Coyote brought it.
In the wettest weather
Rub two sticks together,
Presto—you've got it !

John Vance Cheney.

THE END OF SIR COYOTE.

A FAMOUS fellow was Sir Coyote,
Brimful of pluck and chivalry ;
A regular four-legged knight was he,
The quadrupedal peer of Don Quixote.
This doughty knight of the silver crest,
What wonders he wrought in the far wild West !
Strange that great ones must totter and fall—
Wolseys, Napoleons, Coyotes, and all ;
But it is true
That they do,
And small folk can't help it.—Well,
To the tale the Cahrocs tell :

Sir Coyote, successful from birth,
At length became such a puff
There was not room enough
For him on this little earth ;

A wolf of his size
Must move to the skies.
Now each night came a star
Not so very far
From the hill-top Coyote was wont to sit on,
And a very cute plan his Bigness hit on :
The first good chance,
He would have a dance
With the golden-robed lady.
" To-morrow night," said he,
" I'll hail her, right here by this tree,
And, everything ready,
Forever quit of the vulgar ground,
I'll be at her side in a single bound."

But the keenest earthly craft
May fail in the heavens.   The star,
Holding her course afar,
Only twinkled a little, and laughed
At Coyote's proposal : that's all
The attention she paid to his call.

Now the knight of the silver crest
Swelled so the buttons flew off his vest.
" Ha ! lady," quoth he,
" You defy me.   We'll see."
And he began to bark.
Thereafter every night,
As soon as 'twas dark,
With all his might and main,
Coyote began again :
Bark ! bark ! bark ! *bark !*
The little star,
Shy as our timidest maidens are,
Poor thing ! was so dazed, so distracted
By the shameful manner in which he acted,

That, to end the matter, she promised him square
To lead him next night a round dance in the air.

Coyote, tricked out in his Sunday best,
Was prompt in his place on the peak in the West;
Thence, when the star came up on her round,
He gave a most prodigious bound,
And rearing upright in a manner grand,
Courtly took hold of the lady's hand.
Then for it ! tripping and prancing,
Away they went dancing
Light as a feather,
The star and the wolf together.
Far, far, far, far,
Spun the wolf and the star ;
Into the dim, still sky
Whirled up so high
That the Klaurath, winding slow,
Lay, miles and miles below,
Like a slack bowstring,
Dwindled almost to nothing ;
The valleys looked narrow as threads,
And the Cahroc camps mere arrow-heads.
Higher and higher the dancers flew.
O, how cold, bitter cold, it grew !
Stiffer and stiffer Coyote's knees,
His paws so numb, he could hardly hold.
Cold, cold, O, bitter cold !
Unless there come change of weather,
No help for him—he must freeze.

" Sir Lupus ! Sir Lupus ! we've not come far ;
Cheer up, spin on," cries the rollicking star.
" Mind we foot it together.
Sir Lupus ! Sir Lupus ! look to your knees ;
As you love, Sir Lupus, I pray you don't freeze."

Faster and faster, on and on,
Went the two,
Skipping and dancing,
Tripping and prancing,
Up the blue,
Till Coyote's last hope was gone.
Cold, O, so aching cold !
Frozen from tip of nose
To tips of toes,
At length he—lost his hold.
Then? When? What then?
Back to the earth again
How far it was no one can tell,
But ten long snows, Sir Lupus fell,
A thousand times farther than th' angel in Milton;
And when found, near the spot he was spilt on,
 Sir Coyote lay flat
 As a willow mat.—

It's rather unsafe to dance with a star,
For Coyotes or you, sir, whoever you are.

John Vance Cheney.

FROM "DE ROBERVAL."

ACT II., SCENE VI.

[*Within the Stockade Fort at Quebec. Soldiers carousing.*]

One sings. Fill comrades, fill the bowl right well,
 Trowl round the can with mirth and glee,
 Zip-zip, huzza, Noël ! Noël !
 A health to me, a health to thee,
And Normandie.

Chorus. Pass, comrades, pass the reaming can,
And swig the draught out every man !

Another round as deep as last,
Down to the bottom pig, pardie !
Eyes to the front,—half pikes,—stand fast !
A health to me, a health to thee,
                          And Picardie.

Chorus. Pass, comrades, pass the reaming can,
And swig the draught out every man !

Though this be nought but soldier's tap,
None better wine none ne'er did see,
It riped on our own crofts, mayhap,
So here's a health to thee, to me,
                          An' fair Lorraine,
                               Again—
                                    Lorraine !

Chorus. May he be shot that shirks the can,
Quick, drain the draught out, every man !

[*Enter* OHNAWA ; *soldiers crowd around her.*]

1*st Soldier.* Whom have we here ? This is a shapely
                    wench.
2*nd Soldier.* Clean-limbed.
3*rd Soldier.*   Round-armed.
4*th Soldier.*   Svelte.
5*th Soldier.*   And lithe and lissome.
6*th Soldier.* Like a Provençale in her mumming garb
          On Pope Unreason's day. But where's her dog ?
7*th Soldier.* I saw one like that one in Italy ;
          A statue like her as two peas. They called her
          Bronze something,—I forget. They dug her up,
          And polished her, and set her up on end.

1st Soldier.   Hi, graven image, hast thou ne'er a tongue?
2nd Soldier.   How should she speak but as a magpie
                 chatters?
                 Chat, chat, pretty Mag !
3rd Soldier.   Leave her alone, now.
4th Soldier.   Lay hold on her, and see if she feels warm.

                                [OHNAWA *draws a knife.*]

All.   Aha ! well done ! encore the scene ! well played !

   [ROBERVAL *approaches.   She advances towards him.*]

Soldiers [retiring]. Meat for our master !
Roberval.   Ohnawa !
Ohnawa.   Great Chief.
Rob. What then, my wild fawn, hast indeed come in,
        A live pawn for thy people?   Then I hope
        'Twill be long time ere they make matters up,
        So that we still may keep thee hostage here.
        But say, do practised warriors, shrewd and cunning,
        Send such bright eyes as thine to armed camp,
        To glancing catch full note of our weak points
        Or of our strength?   We hang up spies, Ohnawa.
Ohn. I am no spy.   No warrior sent me here.
Rob. Why did'st thou come?
Ohn.   Did'st thou thyself not ask me?
Rob. I did, i'faith ; and now, thou being here,
        Shalt see such wonders as are to be seen.
        They will impress thy untutored savage mind.
        Notest thou arms upon that slender mast,
        Whose fingers, sudden moving, form new shape?
        By that we speak without the aid of words,
        Long leagues away.
Ohn.   This is not new to me.
        Our braves, on journeys, speak in silent signs
        By leaves, grass, moss, feathers, twigs, and stones.

So that our people can o'ertake the trail,
And tell a message after many moons.

Ro . I've heard of the woodland semaphore.
'Tis a thing to be learned,—and acted on.

Ohn. Why dost thou raise thy head-gear to that blanket?

Reb. Blanket! young savage,—'tis the flag of France,
The far most glorious flag of earth and sea,
That, floating over all this continent,
Shall yet surmount the red brick towers of Spain.
But, pshaw! why do I speak.
              Gunner, fire off a fauconet.
                           [*Gun.*]
What not a wink? Art thou, then, really bronze,
Insensible to wonder?

Ohn.   All is new.

Rob. Then why not show astonishment? Young maids,
When marvels are presented to their view,
Clasp their fore-fingers, or put hand to ears,
Simper, cry "O, how nice!" look down and
    giggle,
And show the perturbation of weak minds.

Ohn. I see new marvels that I ne'er have seen,
But when I once have seen them they are old.

Rob. These are the stables where the chargers are.
             [*Horse led out ; groom gallops.*]
No wonder in thine eyes even at this sight?
Can'st thou look on this steed, and yet not feel
No sight so beautiful in all the world?

Ohn. I have seen herds of these brave gallant beasts.

Rob. [*quicky*] When? where was this?

Ohn.   When that I was a child
A tribe came scouting from the sinking sun,
The hatchet buried, on a pilgrimage
To take salt water back from out the sea,
As is their custom in their solemn rites.
They were all mounted, everyone, on steeds.

Rob. Indeed !

Ohn. Our brethren, who live six moons nearer night,
And many more in number than the stars,
With steeds in number many more than they,
Dwell on the boundless, grassy, hunting-plains,
Beyond which mountains higher than the clouds,
And on the other side of them the sea.

Rob. Important this, but of it more anon.

[*They enter the caserne.*]

These are called books.   These are the strangest
      things
Thou yet hast seen.   I take one of them down,
And lo ! a learned dead man comes from his grave,
Sits in my chair and holds discourse with me.
And these are pictures.

Ohn.   They are good tokens.

Rob. These, maps.

Ohn.   I, with a stick, upon the sand
Can trace the like.

Rob.   By'r Lady of St. Roque
That shalt thou do.   The Pilot missed it there ;
These savages must know their country well.
This girl shall be my chief topographer,
By her I'll learn the gold and silver coast
That Cartier could not find.
Come hither to this window.   Music, ho !

[*Band plays.*]

Art thou not pleased with these melodious sounds ?

Ohn. The small sounds sparkle like a forest fire,
The big horn brays like lowing of the moose,
The undertone is as Niagara.

Rob. Have ye no music, enfans, in the woods ?
No brave high ballad that your warriors sing
To cheer them on a march ?

Ohn.   We have music,
   But our braves sing not.   We have tribal bards
   Who see in dreams things to make music of,
   They tell our squaws, and the good mothers croon
   Them over to their little ones asleep.
Rob. Sing me a forest song, one of thine own.
[OHNAWA *goes to a drum and beats softly with her hand,*
humming the while.]
   This verily is music without words.
   Explain, now, what its purport must mean.
Ohn. The cataracts in the forests have many voices,
   They talk all day and converse beneath the stars,
   The mists hide their faces from the moon.
   The spirits of braves come down from the hunting-
      grounds ;
   They arrive in the night rainbows, and stalk among
      the trees,
   Hearing the voice of the waters.
Rob. Poetic, by my soul.   Why Ohnawa,
   I've found a treasure in thee.   Go now, child ;
               Halt e'er thou goest,
   Here are our wares for trading with the tribes,
   Take something with thee for remembrance,
   Bright scarlet cloth, beads, buttons, rosaries,
   Ribbons and huswifes, scizzors, looking-glasses —
   To civilised and savage women dear.
   Take one, take anything, nay, lade thyself.
   Nothing ?   Shrewd damsel, but that shall not be ;
   No visitor declines a souvenir.
   What hast thou ta'en ?   A dagger double-edged.
   Good, 'tis a choice appropriate, guard it well,
   And hide it in thy corset,—I forget,
   Thou wear'st none.   Go now, girl.   And come again.
                        [*Exeunt.*]

                     J. H. Duvar.

" THE DEATH OF DE SOTO."

ON a shadowy plain where Cypress groves
  And sweeping palm-trees rise,
And the antlered deer, swift-footed, roves,
  The brave De Soto lies.

They have made him a bed, where overhead
  The trailing moss entwines
With leaves of the campion-flower red,
  And gleaming ivy-vines.

Over his fevered forehead creeps,
  From the cedar branches high,
The wind that sleeps in the liquid deeps
  Of the changeless southern sky.

And the Mississippi's turbid tide,
  Broad and free, flows past,
Like the current wide, on which men glide,
  To another ocean vast.

He dreams of the days in sunny Spain,
  When heart and hope were strong,
And he hears again, on the trackless main,
  The sound of the sailor's song.

Now with the fierce Pizarro's band
  ·To wield the sword anew,
He takes command on the golden sand
  Of the shores of proud Peru.

And northward, now, from Tampa Bay,
　With glittering spear and lance,
With pennons gay, and horse's neigh,
　His cohorts brave advance.

Again as the glittering dawn awakes
　From its dreams of purple mist,
By the stoléd priest he kneels and takes
　The holy eucharist.

And the echoing woods and boundless skies
　Are hushed to soft content,
As the strains of the old "Te Deum" rise
　On a new continent.

Again he sees in the thicket damp,
　By the light of a ghastly moon,
The crocodile foul from his native swamp
　Plunge in the dark lagoon.

Again o'er the wide Savannahs flee,
　From his feet, the frightened deer,
And the curlews scream from tree to tree
　Their strange, wild notes of fear.

The wild macaw on her silken nest,
　Mid the orange blossoms white,
From her scarlet breast and golden crest
　Flashes the noonday light.

In the waving grass on the yucca spires,
　Flowers of pallid hue
Blend with the erythrina's fires,
　And the starry nixia's blue.

The rich gordonia blossom swells
  Where the brooklet ripples by,
And the silvery-white halesia bells
  Reflect the cloudless sky.

And southern mosses, soft and brown,
  With gleaming ivies twine,
And heavy purple blooms weigh down
  The wild wistaria vine.

Now on his bold Castilian band
  The native warriors press
From their haunts in the trackless prairie land,
  And the unknown wilderness.

And the flame he has kindled gleams again
  On his sword of trusty steel,
As he burns, mid the yells of savage men,
  Their village of Mobile.

  .   .   .   .   .   .

Like the look of triumph o'er victories won
  That dying conquerors wore,
Or the light that bursts from the setting sun
  On some wild, rugged shore,

The fire of hope lights up anew
  The brave adventurer's brow—
A roseate flash, then death's dull hue—
  And his dream is over now !

So on the plain where Cypress groves
  And spreading palm-trees rise,
And the antlered deer, swift-footed, roves,
  The brave De Soto dies.

                              A. W. Ea'on

TIGER TO TIGRESS.

THE sultry jungle holds its breath ;
The palsied night is dumb as death ;
The golden stars burn large and bland
Above this torrid Indian land ;
But we, that hunger's pangs distress,
Crouch low in deadly watchfulness,
With sleek striped shapes of massive size,
Great velvet paws, and lurid eyes !

Hark ! did you hear that stealthy sound
Where yonder monstrous ferns abound ?
Some lissome leopard pauses there ;
Let him creep nearer, if he dare ! . . .
And hark again ! in yonder grove
I hear that lazy serpent move ;
A mottled thing, whose languid strength
Coils round a bough its clammy length.

Soon the late moon that crimsons air
Will fall with mellow splendour where
The Rajah's distant palace shows
Its haughty domes in dark repose.
And from this dim lair, by-and-by,
We shall behold against pale sky,
With mighty gorges robed in gloom,
The wild, immense Himalayas loom !

At moonrise, through this very spot,
You still remember, do you not,
How that proud Punjaub youth, last night,
Sprang past us on his charger white,

Perchance to have some fair hand throw
A rose from some seraglio ? . . .
Well, if to-night he passes, note
My hot leap at his horse's throat !

A VENGEANCE.

FROM savage pass and rugged shore
The noise of angry hosts had fled ;
The bitter battle raged no more.
Where fiery bolts had wrought their scars,
And where the dying and the dead
In many a woful heap were flung,
While night above the Ægean hung
Its melancholy maze of stars,

One boyish Greek, of princely line,
Lay splashed with blood and wounded sore ;
His wan face in its anguish bore
That delicate symmetry divine,
Carved by the old sculptors of his land.
A broken blade was in his hand,
Half slipping from the forceless hold
That once had swayed it long and well ;
And round his form in tatters fell
The velvet raiment flowered with gold.

But while the calm night later grew,
He heard a stealthy and rustling sound,
Like one who trailed on laggard knee
A shattered shape along the ground.
And soon with sharp surprise he knew
That in the encircling gloom profound

A fierce Turk crawled by slow degrees
To where in helpless pain he lay.
Then, too, he witnessed with dismay
That from the prone Turk's rancorous eye
Flashed the barbaric lurid trace
Of hate's indomitable hell,—
Such hate as death alone could quell,
As death alone could satisfy.

Closer the loitering figure drew,
With naked bosom red from fight,
With ruthless fingers clutching tight
A dagger stained by murderous hue.
Till now, in one great lurch, he threw
His whole frame forward, aiming quick
A deadly inexorable blow,
That weakly faltering, missed its mark,
And left the assassin breathing thick,
Levelled by nerveless overthrow,
There, near the Greek chief, in the dark.
Then he that saw the baffled crime,
Half careless of his life's release,
Since death must win him soon as prey,
Turned on his foe a smile sublime
With pity, and the stars of Greece
Beheld him smile, and only they.

All night the two lay side by side,
Each near to death, yet living each ;
All night the grim Turk moaned and cried,
Beset with pangs of horrid thirst,
Save when his dagger crept to reach,
By wandering ineffectual way,
The prostrate Greek he yearned to slay,
And failure stung him till he cursed.

But when soft prophecies of morn
Had wrapt the sea in wistful white,
A band of men, with faces worn,
Clomb inland past a beetling height,
To find the young chief they adored,
Sought eagerly since fall of sun,
And now in ghastly change restored. . . .
One raised a torch of ruddy shine,
And kneeling by their leader, one
Set-to his mouth a gourd of wine.

Then the young Greek, with wave of hand,
Showed the swart Pagan at his side,
So motioning to the gathered band
That none could.choose but understand—

" Let this man drink ! " he said, and died.

Edgar Fawcett.

THE VOICE OF THE PINE.

'Tis night upon the lake.   Our bed of boughs
Is built where—high above—the pine-tree soughs.
'Tis still,—and yet what woody noises loom
Against the background of the silent gloom !
One well might hear the opening of a flower
If day were hushed as this.   A mimic shower
Just shaken from a branch, how large it sounded,
As 'gainst our canvas roof its three drops bounded !
Across the rumpling waves the hoot-owl's bark
Tolls forth the midnight hour upon the dark.
What mellow booming from the hills doth come ?—
The mountain quarry strikes its mighty drum.

Long had we lain beside our pine-wood fire,
From things of sport our talk had risen higher;
How frank and intimate the words of men
When tented lonely in some forest glen !
No dallying now with masks, from whence emerges
Scarce one true feature forth.   The night-wind urges
To straight and simple speech.   So we had thought
Aloud ; no well-hid secrets but were brought
To light.   The spiritual hopes, the wild,
Unreasoned longings that, from child to child,
Mortals still cherish (though with modern shame),—
To these, and things like these, we gave a name ;
And as we talked, the intense and resinous fire
Lit up the towering boles, till nigh and nigher
They gathered round, a ghostly company,
Like beasts who seek to know what men may be.

Then to our hemlock beds, but not to sleep,—
For listening to the stealthy steps that creep
About the tent or falling branch, but most
A noise was like the rustling of a host,
Or like the sea that breaks upon the shore,—
It was like the pine-tree's murmur.   More and more
It took a human sound.   These words I felt
Into the skyey darkness flood and melt :

" Heardst thou these wanderers reasoning of a time
When men more near the Eternal One shall climb?
How like the new-born child, who cannot tell
A mother's arm that wraps it warm and well !
Leaves of His rose ; drops in His sea that flow,—
Are they, alas, so blind they may not know
Here, in this breathing world of joy and fear,
They can no nearer get to God than here."

R. W. Gilder.

THE WILD RIDE.

I HEAR in my heart, I hear in its ominous pulses
All day, the commotion of sinewy mane-tossing horses ;
All night, from their cells, the importunate tramping and
  neighing.

Let cowards and laggards fall back ! but alert to the
  saddle,
Straight, grim, and abreast, vault our weather-worn
  galloping legion,
With a stirrup-cup each to the one gracious woman that
  loves him.

The road is thro' dolor and dread, over crags and
  morasses ;
There are shapes by the way, there are things that appal
  or entice us :
What odds? We are Knights, and our souls are but
  bent on the riding !

Thought's self is a vanishing wing, and joy is a cobweb,
And friendship a flower in the dust, and glory a sunbeam :
Not here is our prize, nor, alas ! after these our pursuing.

A dipping of plumes, a tear, a shake of the bridle,
A passing salute to this world, and her pitiful beauty !
We hurry with never a word in the track of our fathers.

I hear in my heart, I hear in its ominous pulses
All day, the commotion of sinewy, mane-tossing horses,
All night, from their cells, the importunate tramping and
  neighing.

We spur to a land of no name, out-racing the storm-
wind ;
We leap to the infinite dark, like the sparks from the
anvil,
Thou leadest, O God ! All's well with Thy troopers that
follow.

Louise Imogen Guiney.

THE BALLAD OF HADJI AND THE BOAR.

As I rode over the dusty waste
My dainty Arab's hoof-strokes traced
   Glad rhythms in my mind,
Which seemed to murmur unto me
How he and I were lone and free
   As wide Sahara's wind.

My heart beat high—the sun was bright—
And, as a beacon's startling light
   Proclaims a threatening war,
My burnished lance-point met the glare,
And flashed and sparkled in the air—
   A pale and glancing star.

I saw a hawk pass hovering
Through the azure heights, on balanced wing ;
   Its shadow fell down sheer
Upon my path, then onwards sped,
Smoother than gliding skaters tread
   A fastly-frozen mere.

Thus heedless I, when suddenly
My Hádji broke the reverie
   By stamping on the ground,

Whilst from a brake where grasses rank
Embraced the margin of a tank,
　There came a rustling sound :

No long suspense ;—his bloodshot eyes
Aflame with sullen, fierce surprise—
　Stepped out a grisly boar :
His gloomy aspect seemed to say—
" No other has the right to stray
　Along this marsh-bound shore."

Now I had seen the life-blood gush
From many a boar of nine-inch tusk,
　And so had Hádji too :
But never I ween had we either seen
So great a beast, so gaunt and lean,
　So ugly to the view.

With others by to help at need,
Or give success applausive meed,
　'Tis easy to be brave.
But when a man must do alone,
Each danger seems more dismal grown,
　Each petty ditch a grave.

And so, although the spear-point dropped—
As still as effigy I stopped,
　Nor gave my steed the spur ;
The more I looked, more gruesome grew
This king of all the swinish crew ;
　Mere prudence made demur.

But, as I hung in anguished doubt,
The marsh-born tyrant turned about,
　As weary of the play ;

He turned and dashed adown the glade
(No phantom now or goblin shade),
  The well-known grisly gray :

And doubt no more distressed my mind :
In twenty years I'd never find
  Such trophy to my lance,
For turning he had let me see
His tusks gigantic—shame 'twould be
  If I had lost the chance.

I dropped my hand ; when Hàdji knew
The slackened rein, away he flew
  Across the belt of ooze ;
The slim reeds rustled—till he sprang
Out on the plain whose surface rang
  Beneath his iron shoes.

To left, to right, the wanton shied
At shadows, as in lusty pride
  He rolled his dark fierce eye ;
Or gazing at our grim pursuit
He'd lay his ears back at the brute,
  And snort full savagely.

As minutes came, and lived, and went,
Ever the monster backward sent
  The pebbles in my face,
Yet, when an hour was spent—at length
He seemed to fail in speed and strength,
  And nearer drew the chase.

But lo ! the impetuous Kàvi ran
Before us ; not a means to span
  Its fiercely rushing stream ;

The boar sprang in—we never checked—
And followed ere the foam that flecked
　　His plunge had ceased to gleam.

Above our heads the yellow wave
Triumphant for an instant drave,
　　Then gaping gave us day ;
It gave us day, and snorting loud
Bold Hàdji stemmed the whirling crowd
　　Of surges stopped with spray.

Aboard a skiff two children played,
No little whit were they dismayed
　　To see us swimming boldly ;
One waved his hand in baby glee
When—overboard—most dismally
　　He slipped to perish coldly.

The tender thing sank down below,
I marked its last convulsive throe,
　　But never paused to save.
I would—but just, I chanced to see
The boar bestrew the distant lea
　　With conquered Ràvi's wave.

I turned me from the helpless thing,
I left it darkly struggling,
　　Nor hearkened to my soul ;
I swam beside my gallant steed ;
At length we touched the further reed,
　　And saved a ferry's toll.

But short as seemed the time we'd lost
Long was the space of ground it cost.
　　Not to be covered soon ;

For distant dim the monster grim
Now flitted faint against the rim
    Of the uprising moon.

Yes—like a bubble filled with smoke—
The curd-white moon upswimming broke
    The vacancy of space,
Whilst sinking slowly at my back
The sun breathed blood-stains on the rack
    Which veiled his dying face.

On, on, again ; the snow-fed flood
Had cooled the monster's heated blood,
    And fresh and strong he fled :
An aged peasant crossed his path ;
He turned upon him in his wrath,
    And left him there for dead.

The wretch implored me to remain
And staunch his wound—but all in vain—
    I laughed to see his plight ;
*For I was glad the boar had stayed
To wound the man,* and so delayed
    His headlong rapid flight.

Had Hàdji wearied not a whit,
For stretching free he'd take the bit
    And hold it, or would fling
A foam-flake from his tossing head,
To glitter on his mane's silk thread,
    Whilst ever galloping.

Erelong the arid landscape changed ;
A painter's eye had gladly ranged
    Amidst its varied hue ;—

For far as mortal eye could reach,
As close as pebbles on the beach
  Bright poppy flowers blew.

In countless gaudy chequered squares
Nepenthe grew for human cares—
  Fair dreams for folk who weep,
And multitudes of drowsy bees
Forestalled the dreamy-eyed Chinese,
  Sipping their honied sleep.

All else was silent; not a bird
Disturbed the death of day or stirred
  The calm air with a vesper,
But yet great Nature has her voice,
"Take peace or strife, thou hast the choice,"
  I heard the solemn whisper.

But should I draw my rein for this?
Let dreamers prate of peaceful bliss —
  Such fancies were diseased :
Large sweat-drops trickled from my brow,
The gaping furrows of the plough
  Drank of us and were pleased.

The crimsons of the glowing west
In fainter ruddy shadows dressed
  The mounting eastern moon ;
The slender-pillared palm-tree stems
Were sky-tinged too, as though from gems
  Of garnet they were hewn.

And now when eve had lost its heat,
A Brahmin maiden stole to meet
  Her sweetheart in the dusk ;

Her face adorned each lucid gem
Set round it :—to her garment's hem
  Dripped essences of musk.

Her pensive mien and absent look,
Most plain betrayed a maid forsook
  Of her own gentle heart ;
Outrunning time, she meets her lover,
About her lips dream-kisses hover,
  They smile themselves apart.

"Sah'b! Sah'b!" she sobbed, "I bleed to
    death ! "
The Fates know why—a cruel chance—
No lover's is the fatal glance
  'Neath which the maiden cowers;
No smiling gallant to her tripped,
But in an instant she lies ripped
  And bleeding on the flowers.

" Ah ! give your panting courser breath,
  And call my lover here ! "
But rude and savage passions surged
Within my veins—*I madly urged
  Poor Hádji with the spear.*

And he no longer fought the hand
Which forced his fleetness to command,
  Or snorted to the breeze :
His breaths were choked with piteous sobs,
And I could feel his heart's wild throbs,
  Between my close-set knees.

His glossy coat no longer shone
Red golden as he galloped on,
  And on ! without a check ;

Dank sweat had rusted it to black,
Save where the reins had chafed a track
  Of snow along his neck.

The deepening twilight scarce revealed
Where flights of shadowy night-birds wheeled
  And shrieking greeted us;
But never should my fixéd soul
Forsake the fast-approaching goal,
  For omens timorous.

The jackals woke, and like a rout
Of hell-loosed fiends, their eldritch shout
  Was borne upon the breeze—
Ai! Ai! Ou! Ai!—a ghoulish scream,
And yet half-human; like a dream
  Of mortal agonies.

As I closed in on that evil beast
The champéd froth like creamy yeast
  Bestreaked his grizzled hide;
And like a small and smould'ring brand
His eye back-glancing ever scanned
  Me creeping to his side.

Ha! Ha! He turned to charge and fight;
I shouted out for pure delight,
  And drove my spear-point in.
Clean through his body passed the steel—
I held him off—I made him reel—
  Like chafer on a pin.

An instant so, then through the womb
Of night I galloped, and the gloom
  Of jungles lone and drear :—

But I had stricken, stricken home,
For on my hand his bloody foam
  Had left a purple smear.

So circling back, I peered around,
And, by the moon, too soon I found,
  The grisly brute at bay :
His back was to a thorny tree,
I looked at him, and he at me ;—
  There one of us would stay.

'Twas still as death—we charged together,
And in the dim and sightless weather
  I struck him, but not true :
He seized the lance-shaft in his jaw,
And split it as it were a straw,
  Instead of good bamboo.

Then swift as thought the brute accursed,
Made fiercely in—at Hâdji first—
  Who much disdained to fly :
The little Arab shuddering stood—
Then fell—as monarchs of the wood
  When cruel axes ply.

Ere I could rise, his tusk had cut
All down my back a gaping rut ;—
  He gashed me deep and sore ;
No weapon armed me for the strife,
But rage can fight without a knife,
  I sprang upon the boar.

The thorn stretched out its sable claws,
And nodded with a black applause !
  With fierce sepulchral glee

Three plantains whispered in a rank,
And clapped their fingers long and lank,
  A ghostly gallery.

Above him now—then fallen beneath,
I tore him madly with my teeth,
  Nor loosed my frantic hold ;
One finger searched the spear-head hole,
And dug there like a frightened mole
  'Neath skin and fleshy fold :

I clung around his sinewy crest ;
He leaped, but could not yet divest
  Himself of his alarm.
I hung as close as keepsake locket
On maiden breast—but, from its socket,
  He wrenched my bridle-arm !

No more could I, and with a curse
I yielded to a last reverse,
  And dropped upon the sand.
He glower'd o'er me—then drew back
To make more headlong the attack
  Which nothing should withstand.

But, even then, he chanced to pass
The spot where dying lay—alas !—
  Brave Hàdji—desert-born ;
Not e'en that bristled front was proof
Against the Arab's arméd hoof—
  His brains festooned the thorn.

Then I arose, all dripping red,
And gazed on him I oft had fed,
　And wept to see him low :
No more he'd gallop in his pride—
No mortal man would e'er bestride
　Poor Hâdji here below.

He died amidst those jungles tangled ;
I staggered on all torn and mangled,
　Gasping for painful breath ;
And when, beneath that placid moon,
My spirit left me in a swoon,
　I'd known the worst of death.

Next day they found and bore me home,
And now, they say, I'll never roam
　The glades and forests hoar ;
No more, they say, I'll ever wield
The spear in sport or battle-field,
　Or hunt the grisly boar.

Ian Hamilton.

HAJARLIS.

A Tragic Ballad, set to an old Arabian air.

I LOVED Hajarlis, and was loved,
　Both children of the Desert, we ;
And deep as were her lustrous eyes,
　My image ever could I see :

And in my heart she also shone,
　　As doth a star above a well :
And we each other's thoughts enjoyed,
　　As camels listen to a bell.

A Sheik unto Hajarlis came,
　　And said, "Thy beauty fires my dreams !
Young Ornab spurn—fly to my tent—
　　So shalt thou walk in golden beams."

But from the Sheik my maiden turned,
　　And he was wroth with her, and me ;
Hajarlis down a pit was lowered,
　　And I was fastened to a tree.

Nor bread, nor water, had she there ;
　　But oft a slave would come, and go :
O'er the pit bent he, muttering words—
　　And aye took back the unvarying "No !"

The simoon came with sullen glare !—
　　Breathed desert mysteries through my tree !—
I only heard the starving sighs
　　From that pit's mouth unceasingly.

Day after day—night after night—
　　Hajarlis' famished moans I hear !
And then I prayed her to consent—
　　For *my* sake, in my wild despair.

Calm strode the Sheik—looked down the pit,
　　And said, "Thy beauty now is gone :
Thy last moans will thy lover hear,
　　While thy slow torments feed my scorn."

They spared me that I still might know
Her thirst and frenzy—till at last
The pit was silent !—and I felt
Her life—and mine—were with the past !

A friend, that night, cut through my bonds :
The Sheik amidst his camels slept ;—
We fired his tent, and drove them in—
And then with joy I scream'd and wept !

And cried, " A spirit comes arrayed,
From that dark pit, in golden beams !
Thy slaves are fled—thy camels mad -
Hajarlis once more fires thy dreams ! "

The camels blindly trod him down,
While still we drove them o'er his bed ;
Then with a stone I beat his breast,
As I would smite him ten times dead !

I dragg'd him far out on the sands—
And vultures came—a screaming shoal !—
And while they fang'd and flapp'd, I prayed
Great Allah to destroy his soul !

And day and night, again I sat
Above that pit, and thought I heard
Hajarlis' moans—and cried, " My love ! "
With heart still breaking at each word.

Is it the night-breeze in my ear,
That woos me, like a fanning dove ?—
Is it herself?—O, desert-sands,
Enshroud me ever with my love !

R. Hengist Horne.

THE FAIR OF ALMACHÀRA.

" A Delineation of the great Fair of Almachàra, in Arabia,
which, to avoid the great heat of the sun, is kept in the
night, and by the light of the moon."—SIR THOMAS BROWNE'S
Musœum Clausum.

I.

THE intolerant sun sinks down with glaring eye
  Behind the horizontal desert line,
And upwards casts his robes to float on high,
  Suffusing all the clouds with his decline ;
  Till their intense gold doth incarnadine,
And melt in angry hues, which darken as they die.

Slow rose the naked beauty of the Moon
  In broad relief against the gloomy vault :
Each smouldering field in azure melted soon,
  Before the tenderness of that assault ;
  And the pure Image that men's souls exalt,
Stood high aloof from earth, as in some vision'a swoon.

But now she seem'd, from that clear altitude,
  To gaze below, with a far-sheening smile,
On Arab tents, gay groups, and gambols rude,
  As in maternal sympathy the while ;
  And now, like swarming bees, o'er many a mile
Forth rush the swarthy forms o' the gilded multitude !

II.

Hark to the cymbals singing !
Hark to their hollow gust !
The gong sonorous singing
At each sharp pistol-shot !

Bells of sweet tone are ringing !
    The Fair begins
    With countless dins,
And many a grave-faced plot !—

Trumpets and tympans sound
'Neath the moon's brilliant round,
    Which doth entrance
    Each passionate dance,
    And glows or flashes
    Midst jewell'd sashes,
Cap, turban, and tiàra,
    In a tossing sea
    Of ecstasy,
At the Fair of Almachàra !

III.

First came a troop of Dervishes,
    Who sang a solemn song,
And at each chorus one leapt forth
    And spun himself so long
That silver coins, and much applause,
    Were shower'd down by the throng.

Then pass'd a long and sad-link'd chain
    Of foreign Slaves for sale :
Some clasp'd their hands and wept like rain,
    Some with resolve were pale ;
By death or fortitude, they vow'd,
    Deliverance should not fail.

And neighing steeds with bloodshot eyes,
    And tails as black as wind

That sweeps the storm-expectant seas,
Bare-back'd, career'd behind ;
Yet, docile to their master's call,
Their steep-arch'd necks inclined.

Trumpets and tympans sound
'Neath the moon's brilliant round,
Which doth entrance
Each passionate dance,
And glows or flashes
'Mid cymbal-clashes,
Rich jewell'd sashes,
Cap, turban, and tiàra,
In a tossing sea
Of ecstasy,
At the Fair of Almachàra !

IV.

There sit the Serpent-charmers,
Enwound with maze on maze
Of orby folds, which, working fast,
Puzzle the moon-lit gaze.
Boas and amphisbœnæ gray
Flash like currents in their play,
Hissing and kissing, till the crowd
Shriek with delight, or pray aloud !

Now rose a crook-back'd Juggler,
Who clean cut off both legs ;
Astride on his shoulders set them,
Then danced on wooden pegs :
And presently his head dropp'd off,
When another juggler came,

Who gathered his frisky fragments up
And stuck them in a frame,—
From which he issued as at first,—
Continuing thus the game.

Trumpets and tympans sound
'Neath the moon's brilliant round,
    Which doth entrance
    Each passionate dance,
    And glows or flashes
    'Mid cymbal clashes,
    Rich jewell'd sashes,
Cap, turban, and tiàra,
    In a tossing sea
    Of ecstasy,
At the Fair of Almachàra !

                v.

There do we see the Merchants
    Smoking with grave pretence ;
There, too, the humble dealers,
    In cassia and frankincense ;
And many a Red-Sea mariner,
    Swept from its weedy waves,
Who comes to sell his coral rough,
    Torn from its rocks and caves,—
With red clay for the potteries,
    That careful baking craves.

There, too, the Bedouin Tumblers
    Roll round like rapid wheels ;
Or tie their bodies into knots,
    Hiding both head and heels :

Now standing on each other's heads,
　They race about the Fair,
Or with strange energies inspired,
　Leap high into the air,
And wanton thus above the sand,
　In graceful circles rare.

There sit the Opium-eaters,
　Chanting their gorgeous dreams ;
While some, with hollow faces,
　Seem lit by ghastly gleams,—
Dumb—and with fixed grimaces !

There dance the Arab maidens,
　With burnish'd limbs all bare,
Caught by the moon's keen silver,
　Through frantic jets of hair !
O, naked Moon !　O, wondrous face !
Eternal sadness—beauty—grace—
Smile on the passing human race !

Trumpets and tympans sound
'Neath the moon's brilliant round,
　　Which doth entrance
　　Each passionate dance,
　　And glows or flashes
　　'Mid cymbal clashes,
　　Rich jewelled sashes,
Cap, turban, and tiàra,
　　In a tossing sea
　　Of ecstasy,
At the Fair of Almachàra !

VI.

There, too, the Story-tellers,
  With long beards and bald pates,
Right earnestly romancing
  Grave follies of the Fates;
For which their circling auditors
  Throw coins and bags of dates.
Some of the youths and maidens shed
  Sweet tears, or turn quite pale;
But silence, and the clouded pipe,
  O'er all the rest prevail.

Mark yon Egyptian Sorcerer,
  In black and yellow robes!
His ragged raven locks he twines
  Around two golden globes!
And now he lashes a brazen gong,
Whirling about with shriek and song;
  Till the globes burst in fire,
  Which, in a violet spire,
Shoots o'er the loftiest tent-tops there,
Then fades away in perfume rare;
With music somewhere in the sky—
Whereat the Sorcerer seems to die!

Broad cymbals are clashing,
And flying and flashing!
And spinning and pashing!
The silver bells ringing!
All tingling and dingling!
Gongs booming and swinging!
The Fair's at its height
In the cool brilliant night!

While streams the Moon's glory
 On javelins and sabres,
And long beards all hoary ;
 Midst trumpets and tabors,—
Wild strugglings and trammels
Of leaders and camels
And horsemen, in masses,
Midst droves of wild asses,—
The clear beams entrancing,
The passionate dancing,
Glaring fixt, or in flashes,
From jewels in sashes,
 Cap, turban, tiàra ;—
  'Tis a tossing sea
  Of ecstasy,
At the Fair of Almachàra !

R. Hengist Horne.

FROM "ARCTIC HEROES."

SCENE, a stupendous region of icebergs and snow. The bare mast of a half-buried ship stands among the rifts and ridges. The figures of Two Men,* covered closely with furs and skins, slowly emerge from beneath the winter housing of the deck, and descend upon the snow by an upper ladder, and steps cut below in the frozen wall of snow. They advance upon the ice.

1*st Man*. We are out of hearing now : give thy heart words.

[*They walk in silence some steps further, and then pause.*]

* The "Two Men" are supposed to be Sir John Franklin and his First Lieutenant

2nd Man. Here 'midst the sea's unfathomable ice,
Life-piercing cold and the remorseless night
Which blinds our thoughts, nor changes its dead
    face,
Save in the 'ghast smile of the hopeless moon,
Must slowly close our sum of wasted hours,
And with them all the enterprising dreams,
Efforts, endurance, and resolve which make
The power and glory of us Englishmen.
1st Man.   It may be so.
2nd Man. Oh, doubt not but it must.
Day after day, week crawling after week,
So slowly that they scarcely seem to move,
Nor we to know it till our calendar,
Shows us that months have lapsed away, and left
Our drifting time while here our bodies lie,
Like melancholy blots upon the snow.
Thus have we lived, and gradually seen
By calculations which appear to mock
Our hearts with their false figures, that 'tis now
Three years since we were cut off from the world,
By these impregnable walls of solid ocean !
1st Man. All this is true : the physical elements
We fought to conquer, are too strong for us.
2nd Man. We have felt the crush of battle side by side ;
Seen our best friends, with victory in their eyes,
Suddenly smitten down, a mangled heap,
And thought our own turn might be next ; yet never
Drooped we in spirit, or such horror felt
As in the voiceless torture of this place
Which freezes up the mind.
1st Man. Not yet.
2nd Man. I feel it.
Death, flying red-eyed from the cannon's mouth,
Were child's play to confront, compared with this ;
Inch by inch famished in the silent frost,

The cold anatomies of our dear friends,
One by one carried in their rigid sheets
To lie beneath the snow, till he that's last
Creeps to the lonely horror of his berth
Within the vacant ship ; and while the bears
Grope round and round, thinks of his distant home,
Those dearest to him—glancing rapidly
Through his past life—then, with a wailful sigh,
And a brief prayer, his soul becomes a blank.

1st Man. This is despair : I'll hear no more of it.
We have provisions still.

2nd Man. And for how long ?

1st Man. A flock of wild birds may pass over us,
And some our shots may reach.

2nd Man. And by this chance
Find food for one day more.

1st Man. Yes, and thank God ;
For preservation the next day may come,
And rescue from Old England.

2nd Man. All our fuel
Is nearly gone ; and as the last log burns,
And falls in ashes, so may we foresee
The frozen circle sitting round.

1st Man. Nay, nay——

2nd Man. Have we not burnt bulkhead, partition, door,
Till one grim family, with glassy eyes
And hollow voices, crouch beneath the deck,
Which soon—our only safeguard—we must burn ?

1st Man. Our boats, loose spars, our masts—the fore-
        castle—
Must serve us ere that pass.   But if indeed
Nothing avail, and no help penetrate
To this remote place, inaccessible
Perchance for years, except to some wild bird--
Or creature, stranger than the crimson snow—
We came here knowing all this might befall,

And set our lives at stake.   God's will be done.
I, too, have felt the horrors of our fate ;
Jammed in a moving field of solid ice,
Borne onward day and night we knew not where,
Till the loud cracking sounds reverberating
Far distant, were soon followed by the rending
Of the vast pack, whose heaving blocks and wedges
Like crags broke loose, all rose to our destruction,
As by some ghastly instinct.   Then the hand
Of winter smote the all-congealing air,
And with its freezing tempest piled on high
These massy fragments which environ us,—
Cathedrals many-spired, by lightning riven ;
Sharp-angled chaos-heaps of palaced cities ;
With splintered pyramids and broken towers,
That yawn for ever at the bursting moon,
And her four pallid flame-spouts :—now, appalled
By the long roar of the cloud-like avalanche,—
Now, by the stealthy creeping of the glaciers
In silence to'ards our frozen ships.   So Death
Hath often whispered to me in the night,
And I have seen him on the Aurora-gleam,
Smile as I rose and came upon the deck ;
Or when the icicle's prismatic glance
Bright, flashing—and then, colourless, unmoved ice,
Emblem'd our passing life, and its cold end.
O, friend in many perils, fail not now !
Am I not, e'en as thou art, utterly sick
Of my own heavy heart, and loading clothes ?
A mind, that in its firmest hour, hath fits
Of madness for some change, that shoot across
Its steadfastness, and scarce are trampled down :
Yet, friend, I will not let my spirit sink,
Nor shall mine eyes, e'en with snow-blindness
    veiled,
Man's great prerogative of inward sight

Forego, nor cease therein to speculate
On England's feelings for her countrymen ;
Whereof relief will some day surely come.
2nd Man. I well believe it ; but, I feel, too late.
1st Man. Then, if too late, one noble task remains,
And one consoling thought : we, to the last,
With firmness, order, and considerate care,
Will act as though our death-beds were at home,
Grey heads with honour sinking to the tomb ;
So future ages shall record that we,
Imprisoned in these frozen horrors, held
Our sense of duty, both to man and God.

[*The muffled beat of the ship's bell sounds for evening prayers.*]

[*The Two Men return ; they ascend the steps in the snow — then the ladder—and disappear beneath the snow-covered housing of the deck.*]

R. Hengist Horne.

THE MAID OF THE BENI YEZID.

ZULEIKA ! The Turk ! ! Zuleika, stand forth,
  If Arab you are to the core ;
By the east, by the north
Euphrates down-pour'th,
  To the west is the marsh without shore.

Zuleika, be swift ! Zuleika, our tents
  Are girt by deep marshes and foes ;
To the south like a fence,
A squadron immense
  Of Turks, while we slumbered, arose !

" Up, maid of the desert !   If still the old stamp
　　Lingers on in the seed of Yezid,
Deck your charms without lamp
And list for the tramp
　　Of the mare never stranger has rid.

" You shall lead on our charge in the wild Arab way,
　　You shall rally the young men and old,
Like the hawk or the jay
We shall cleave through the fray :
　　Your death by the bards shall be told."

With pride, with delight, after old Arab wont
　　For a bridal she decks her sweet form.
To the fore, to the front,
To the battle's quick brunt
　　She is whirling the keen desert swarm.

When first on Euphrates the thousand-edged sword
　　Of the sun the fog-serpent had gashed,
With one man's accord
The whole Arab horde
　　On their foe like a thunderbolt crashed.

Then vain were the cannon of Omar the Turk,
　　Sword or pistol-flash—onward they raced !
Short, sharp is the work,
In the dust column's murk
　　Are vanished the sons of the waste.

But Zuleika ?   Alas, the mare is too frail
　　That swerves from the cannon aside !
As birds on the gale
Are caught in the sail,
　　Entrapped is the desert's fair bride.

She has played, she has lost.   With a firm pallid face
  By Omar the wrathful she stands ;
"Dread lord, grant me grace
That here in this place
  Undefiled I may die by your hands !"

Then still is each pulse, while Omar his brow
  Rubs clear of the wrinkles and cries :
"Not so, for I vow
That in Bagdad enow
  Of the ladies shall welcome this prize !

"Fair bloom of the desert, a princess's train
  And honours henceforth you shall boast ;
When the year comes again
To the season of rain
  Choose your mate from the best of my host."

Zuleika says naught, but far o'er the plain
  Her heart follows after her kin,
From the eyes of disdain
Her tears ever rain
  As to Bagdad the horsemen ride in.

When the year turned again, was Zuleika a bride ?
  With a Turk the proud maid would not mate.
Like a queen in her pride
To the desert they ride ;
  All the city looks on from the gate.

Her tribesmen have come from the tents of the free
  For the maid they had mourned as a slave ;
By each gay saddle tree
All Bagdad may see
  How Turks love to honor the brave.

" Farewell, noble Omar, and Bagdad, farewell !
Your pleasures are not to our taste ;
In the close town to dwell
For an Arab is hell—
We must wed, live, and die in the waste !"

Charles De Kay.

THE REVENGE OF HAMISH.

IT was three slim does and a ten-tined buck in the bracken
   lay;
And all of a sudden the sinister smell of a man,
Awaft on a wind-shift, wavered and ran
Down the hill-side, and sifted along through the bracken
   and passed that way.

Then Nan got a-tremble at nostril ; she was the daintiest
   doe ;
In the print of her velvet flank on the velvet fern
She reared, and rounded her ears in turn.
Then the buck leapt up, and his head as a king's to a
   crown did go,

Full high in the breeze, and he stood as if Death had the
   form of a deer ;
And the two slim does long lazily stretching arose,
For their day-dream slowlier came to a close,
Till they woke and were still, breath-bound with waiting
   and wonder and fear.

Then Alan, the huntsman, sprang over the hillock, the
   hounds shot by,
The does and the ten-tined buck made a marvellous
   bound,

The hounds swept after with never a sound,
But Alan loud winded his horn in sign that the quarry
was nigh.

For at dawn of that day proud Maclean of Lochbuy to
the hunt had waxed wild,
And he cursed at old Alan till Alan fared off with the
hounds
For to drive him the deer to the lower glen-grounds :
" I will kill a red deer," quoth Maclean, " in the sight of
the wife and the child."

So gayly he faced with the wife and the child to his
chosen stand :
But he hurried tall Hamish, the henchman, ahead :
" Go turn,"—
Cried Maclean—" if the deer seek to cross to the burn,
Do thou turn them to me ; nor fail, lest thy back be red
as thy hand."

Now hard-fortuned Hamish, half-blown of his breath with
the height of the hill,
Was white in the face when the ten-tined buck and the
does
Drew leaping to burn-ward ; huskily rose
His shouts, and his nether lip twitched and his legs were
o'er-weak for his will.

So the deer darted lightly by Hamish, and bounded
away to the burn.
But Maclean never bating his watch tarried waiting
below.
Still Hamish hung heavy with fear for to go
All the space of an hour ; then he went, and his face was
greenish and stern,

And his eyes sat back in the socket, and shrunken the
   eyeballs shone,
As withdrawn from a vision of deeds it were shame to
   see.
" Now, now, grim henchman, what is't with thee ? "
Brake Maclean, and his wrath rose red as a beacon the
   wind hath upblown.

" Three does and a ten-tined buck made out," spoke
   Hamish, full mild,
" And I ran for to turn, but my breath it was blown,
   and they passed ;
I was weak, for ye called ere I broke me my fast."
Cried Maclean : " Now a ten-tined buck in the sight of
   the wife and the child

" I had killed if the gluttonous kern had not wrought me
   a snail's own wrong ! "
Then he sounded, and down came kinsmen and clansmen all :
" Ten blows, for ten tine, on his back let fall,
And reckon no stroke if the blood follow not at the
   bite of the thong ! "

So Hamish made bare, and took him his strokes ; at the
   last he smiled.
" Now, I'll to the burn," quoth Maclean, " for it still
   may be,
If a slimmer-paunched henchman will hurry with me,
I shall kill me the ten-tined buck for a gift to the wife
   and the child ! "

Then the clansmen departed, by this path and that ; and
   over the hill
Sped Maclean with an outward wrath for an inward
   shame ;

And that place of the lashing full quiet became ;
And the wife and the child stood sad ; and the bloody-
backed Hamish sat still.

But look 1 red Hamish has risen ; quick about and about
turns he.
" There is none betwixt me and the crag-top 1 " he
screams under breath.
Then livid as Lazarus lately from death,
He snatches the child from the mother, and clambers the
crag toward the sea.

Now the mother drops breath ; she is dumb, and her
heart goes dead for a space,
Till the motherhood, mistress of death, shrieks, shrieks
through the glen,
And that place of the lashing is live with men,
And Maclean, and the gillie that told him, dash up in a
desperate race.

Not a breath's time for asking ; an eye-glance reveals all
the tale untold.
They follow mad Hamish afar up the crag toward the
sea,
And the lady cries : " Clansmen, run for a fee !—
Yon castle and lands to the two first hands that shall
hook him and hold

Fast Hamish back from the brink ! "—and ever she flies
up the steep,
And the clansmen pant, and they sweat, and they
jostle and strain,
But, mother, 'tis vain ; but, father, 'tis vain ;
Stern Hamish stands bold on the brink, and dangles the
child o'er the deep.

Now a faintness falls on the men that run, and they all
  stand still.
And the wife prays Hamish as if he were God, on her
  knees,
Crying: "Hamish! O Hamish! but please, but
  please
For to spare him!" and Hamish still dangles the child
  with a wavering will.

On a sudden he turns; with a sea-hawk scream, and a
  gibe, and a song,
Cries: "So; I will spare ye the child if, in sight of
  ye all,
Ten blows on Maclean's bare back shall fall,
And ye reckon no stroke if the blood follow not at the
  bite of the thong!"

Then Maclean he set hardly his tooth on his lip that his
  tooth was red,
Breathed short for space, said: "Nay, but it never
  shall be!
Let me hurl off the damnable hound in the sea!"
But the wife: "Can Hamish go fish us the child from
  the sea, if dead?

Say yea!—Let them lash *me*, Hamish?"—"Nay!"—
  "Husband, the lashing will heal;
But, oh, who will heal me the bonny sweet bairn in
  his grave?
Could ye cure me my heart with the death of a knave?
Quick! Love! I will bare thee—so—kneel!" Then
  Maclean 'gan slowly to kneel.

With never a word, till presently downward he jerked to
  the earth.
Then the henchman—he that smote Hamish—would
  tremble and lag;

"Strike hard !" quoth Hamish, full stern, from the
    crag ;
Then he struck him, and "One !" sang Hamish, and
danced with the child in his mirth.

And no man spake beside Hamish ; he counted each
    stroke with a song.
    When the last stroke fell, then he moved him a pace
        down the height,
    And he held forth the child in the heartaching sight
Of the mother, and looked all pitiful grave, as repenting
    a wrong.

And there as the motherly arms stretched out with the
    thanksgiving prayer—
    And there as the mother crept up with a fearful swift
        pace,
    Till her finger nigh felt of the bairnie's face—
In a flash fierce Hamish turned round and lifted the
    child in the air,

And sprang with the child in his arms from the horrible
    height in the sea,
    Shrill screeching, "Revenge !" in the wind-rush ;
        and pallid Maclean,
    Age-feeble with anger and impotent pain,
Crawled up on the crag, and lay flat, and locked hold of
    dead roots of a tree—

And gazed hungrily o'er, and the blood from his back
    drip-dripped in the brine,
    And a sea-hawk flung down a skeleton fish as he flew,
    And the mother stared white on the waste of blue,
And the wind drove a cloud to seaward, and the sun
    began to shine.

                                    Sidney Lanier.

THE PASSING OF CLOTE SCARP.

[Clote Scarp is the legendary hero of the Melicites, the same as Gluscâp of the Micmacs.]

STILL in the Indian lodges
  Is the old story told,—
How Clote Scarp's passing ended
  Acadia's Age of Gold.

—In the primeval forest—
  In the old happy days,
The men and beasts lived peaceful
  Among the woodland ways ;—

The forest knew no spoiler ;
  —No timid beast or bird
Knew fang or spear or arrow ;—
  No cry of pain was heard ;—

For all loved gentle Clote Scarp,
  And Clote Scarp loved them all,
And men and beasts and fishes
  Obeyed his welcome call :

—The birds came circling round him
  With carols fresh and sweet ;
The little wilding blossoms
  Sprang up about his feet ;—

All spake one simple language,
  And Clote Scarp understood,
And, in his tones of music,
  Taught them that Love was good !

   •   ᴗ   ◼   •   •

But, in the course of ages,
   An alien spirit woke,
And men and woodland creatures
   Their peaceful compact broke ;--

Then,—through the gloomy forest,
   The hunter tracked his prey,
The bear and wolf went roaming
   To ravage and to slay ;—

Through the long reeds and grasses
   Stole out the slimy snake,
The hawk pounced on the birdling
   Close nestling in the brake ;—

The beaver built his stronghold
   Beneath the river's flow,
The partridge sought the coverts
   Where beeches thickest grow ;

In pain and trembling terror
   Each timid creature fled
To seek a safer refuge
   And hide its hunted head !

      .   .   .   .   .

In sorrow and in anger
   Then gentle Clote Scarp spake :
" My soul can bear no longer
   The havoc that ye make ;

Ye will not heed my bidding,
   —I cannot stay your strife ;
And so I needs must leave you
   Till Love renew your life ! "

Then, by the great, wide water,
He spread a parting feast ;
—The men refused his bidding,
But there came bird and beast ;

There came the bear and walrus,
—The wolf, with bristling crest,
—There came the busy beaver,
—The deer, with bounding breast ;

There came the mink and otter,
The seal, with wistful eyes,
The birds, in countless numbers
With sad imploring cries !

And, when the feast was over,
He launched his bark canoe ;—
The wistful creatures watched him
Swift gliding from their view ;—

They heard his far-off singing
Through the fast-falling night,
Till, on the dim horizon,
He vanished from their sight ;

And then, a wail of sorrow
Went up from one and all ;
Then echoed through the twilight
The Loon's long mournful call.

Still through the twilight echoes
That cadence wild and shrill,
But, in a blessèd island,
Clote Scarp is waiting still ;

495

No cold or dark or tempest
Comes near that happy spot ;
It fears no touch of winter
For winter's self is not !

And there is Clote Scarp waiting
Till happier days shall fall,
Till strife be fled for ever,
And Love be Lord of all !

Agnes Maude Machar.

BENDOURAIN, THE OTTER MOUNT.

(*From the Gaelic.*)

"Bendourain is a forest scene in the wilds of Glenorchy. The poem, or lay, is descriptive, less of the forest, or its mountain fastnesses, than of the habits of the creatures that tenant the locality—the dun-deer and the roe. So minutely enthusiastic is the hunter's treatment of his theme, that the attempt to win any favour for his performance from the Saxon reader is attended with no small risk. The composition is always rehearsed or sung to pipe music, of which it is considered, by those who understand the original, a most extraordinary echo, besides being in other respects a very powerful specimen of Gaelic minstrelsy."—*Scottish Minstrelsy.*

Urlar.

THE noble Otter hill !
 It is a chieftain Beinn,*
Ever the fairest still
 Of all these eyes have seen.
Spacious is his side ;
I love to range where hide,

* Anglicised into *Ben.*

In haunts by few espied,
    The nurslings of his den.
In the bosky shade
Of the velvet glade,
Couch, in softness laid,
    The nimble-footed deer ;
To see the spotted pack,
That in scenting never slack,
Coursing on their track,
    Is the prime of cheer.
Merry may the stag be,
    The lad that so fairly
Flourishes the russet coat
    That fits him so rarely.
'Tis a mantle whose wear
Time shall not tear ;
'Tis a banner that ne'er
    Sees its colours depart :
And when they seek his doom,
Let a man of action come,
A hunter in his bloom,
    With rifle not untried :
A notch'd, firm fasten'd flint,
To strike a trusty dint,
And make the gun-lock glint
    With a flash of pride.
Let the barrel be but true,
And the stock be trusty too,
So, Lightfoot,* though he flew,
    Shall be purple-dyed.
He should not be novice bred,
But a marksman of first head,
By whom that stag is sped,
    In hill-craft not unskill'd ;

* The deer.

So, when Padraig of the glen
Call'd his hounds and men,
The hill spake back again,
   As his orders shrill'd ;
Then was firing snell,
And the bullets rain'd like hail,
And the red-deer fell
   Like warrior on the field.

Siubhal.

Oh, the young doe so frisky,
   So coy, and so fair,
That gambols so briskly,
   And snuffs up the air ;
And hurries, retiring,
To the rocks that environ,
When foemen are firing,
   And bullets are there.
Though swift in her racing,
   Like the kinsfolk before her,
No heart-burst, unbracing
   Her strength, rushes o'er her.
'Tis exquisite hearing
Her murmur, as, nearing,
Her mate comes careering,
   Her pride, and her lover ;—
He comes—and her breathing
   Her rapture is telling ;
How his antlers are wreathing,
   His white haunch, how swelling !
High chief of Bendourain,
He seems, as adoring
His hind, he comes roaring
   To visit her dwelling.

'Twere endless my singing
How the mountain is teeming
With thousands, that bringing
    Each a high chief's* proud seeming,
With his hind, and her gala
Of younglings, that follow
O'er mountain and beala,†
    All lightsome are beaming.
When that lightfoot so airy,
    Her race is pursuing,
Oh, what vision saw e'er a
    Feat of flight like her doing?
She springs, and the spreading grass
Scarce feels her treading,
It were fleet foot that sped in
    Twice the time that she flew in.
The gallant array!
    How the marshes they spurn,
In the frisk of their play,
    And the wheeling they turn,—
As the cloud of the mind
They would distance behind,
And give years to the wind,
    In the pride of their scorn !
'Tis the marrow of health
    In the forest to lie,
Where, nooking in stealth,
    They enjoy her‡ supply,—
Her fosterage breeding
A race never needing,

* Stag of the first head.   † Pass.
‡ Any one who has heard a native attempt the Lowland
tongue for the first time is familiar with the personification
that turns every inanimate object into *he* or *she.* The forest is
here happily personified as a nurse or mother.

Save the milk of her feeding,
   From a breast never dry.
Her hill-grass they suckle,
   Her mammets they swill,
And in wantonness chuckle
   O'er tempest and chill,
With their ankles so light,
And their girdles of white,
And their bodies so bright
   With the drink of the rill.
Through the grassy glen sporting
   In murmurless glee,
Nor snow-drift nor fortune
   Shall urge them to flee,
Save to seek their repose
In the clefts of the knowes,
And the depths of the howes
   Of their own Eas-an-ti.*

Urlar.

In the forest den, the deer
Makes, as best befits, her lair,
Where is plenty, and to spare,
   Of her grassy feast.
There she browses free
On herbage of the lea,
Or marsh grass, daintily,
   Until her haunch is greased.
Her drink is of her well,
Where the water-cresses swell,
Nor with the flowing shell
   Is the toper better pleased.

* *Gaelic*—Easan-an-tsith.

The bent makes nobler cheer,
Or the rashes of the mere,
Then all the creagh that e'er
   Gave surfeit to a guest.
Come, see her table spread ;
The *sorach* * sweet display'd,
The *ealvi*,† and the head
   Of the daisy stem ;
The *dorach*‡ crested, sleek,
And ringed with many a streak,
Presents her pastures meek,
   Profusely by the stream.
Such the luxuries
That plump their noble size,
And the herd entice
   To revel in the howes.
Nobler haunches never sat on
Pride of grease, than when they batten
On the forest links, and fatten
   On the herbs of their carouse.
Oh, 'tis pleasant, in the gloaming,
   When the supper-time
Calls all their hosts from roaming,
   To see their social prime ;
And when the shadows gather,
They lair on native heather,
Nor shelter from the weather
   Need, but the knolls behind.
Dread or dark is none ;
Their's the mountain throne,
Height and slope their own,
   The gentle mountain kind ;
Pleasant is the grace

* Sorrel.   † St. John's-wort.
‡ A kind of cress or marsh-mallow.

Of their hue and dappled dress,
And an ark in their distress,
  In Bendourain dear they find.

Siubhal.

So brilliant thy hue
  With tendril and flow'ret,
The grace of the view,
  What land can o'erpower it ?
Thou mountain of beauty,
Methinks it might suit thee,
The homage of beauty
  To claim as a queen.
What needs it ? Adoring
Thy reign, we see pouring
The wealth of their store in
  Already, I ween.
The seasons—scarce roll'd,
The r gifts are twice told—
And the months, they unfold
  On thy bosom their dower,
With profusion so rare,
Ne'er was clothing so fair,
Nor was jewelling e'er
  Like the bud and the flower
Of the groves on thy breast,
Where rejoices to rest
His magnificent crest,
  The mountain-cock, shrilling
In quick time, his note;
And the clans of the grot
With melody's note,
  Their numbers are trilling.
No foot can compare,
  In the dance of the green,

With the roebuck's young heir;
And here he is seen.
Should hurry on the fallow deer,
   But steal on her with caution ;—
With wary step and watchfulness
To stalk her to her resting-place,
Insures the gallant wight's success,
   Before she is in motion.
The hunter bold should follow then,
By bog, and rock, and hollow, then,
And nestle in the gully, then,
And watch with deep devotion
The shadows on the benty grass,
And how they come, and how they pass ;
Nor must he stir, with gesture rash,
   To quicken her emotion.
With nerve and eye so wary, sir,
That straight his piece may carry, sir,
He marks with care the quarry, sir,
   The muzzle to repose on ;
And now, the knuckle is applied,
The flint is struck, the priming tried,
Is fired, the volley has replied,
   And reeks in high commotion ;—
Was better powder ne'er to flint,
Nor trustier wadding of the lint—
And so we strike a telling dint,
   Well done, my own Nic-Coisean !*

Duncan Ban Macintyre.

* Literally—" From the barrel of Nic-Coisean." This was the
poet's favourite gun, to which his muse has addressed a
separate song of considerable merit.

THE SONG OF WINTER.

(*From the Gaelic.*)

This is selected as a specimen of Mackay's descriptive poetry. It is in a style peculiar to the Highlands, where description runs so entirely into epithets and adjectives, as to render recitation breathless, and translation hopeless. Here, while we have retained the imagery, we have been unable to find room, or rather rhyme, for one half of the epithets in the original. The power of alliterative harmony in the original song is extraordinary.

I.

AT waking so early
    Was snow on the Ben,
And, the glen of the hill in,
The storm-drift so chilling
The linnet was stilling,
    That couch'd in its den ;
And poor robin was shrilling
    In sorrow his strain.

II.

Every grove was expecting
    Its leaf shed in gloom ;
The sap it is draining,
Down rootwards 'tis straining
And the bark it is waning
    As dry as the tomb,
And the blackbird at morning
    Is shrieking his doom.

III.

Ceases thriving, the knotted,
    The stunted birk-shaw ;*

* "Birk-shaw." A few Scotticisms will be found in these versions, at once to flavour the style, and, it must be admitted, to assist the rhymes.

While the rough wind is blowing,
And the drift of the snowing
Is shaking, o'erthrowing,
　The copse on the law.

IV.

'Tis the season when nature
　Is all in the sere,
When her snow-showers are hailing,
Her rain-sleet assailing,
Her mountain winds wailing,
　Her rime-frosts severe.

V.

'Tis the season of leanness,
　Unkindness, and chill;
Its whistle is ringing,
An iciness bringing,
Where the brown leaves are clinging
　In helplessness, still,
And the snow-rush is delving
　With furrows the hill.

VI.

The sun is in hiding,
　Or frozen its beam
On the peaks where he lingers,
On the glens, where the singers,*
With their bills and small fingers
　Are raking the stream,
Or picking the midstead
　For forage—and scream.

* Birds.

VII.

When darkens the gloaming
  Oh, scant is their cheer !
All benumb'd is their song in
The hedge they are thronging,
And for shelter still longing,
    The mortar* they tear ;
Ever noisily, noisily
  Squealing their care.

VIII.

The running stream's chieftain†
  Is trailing to land,
So flabby, so grimy, —
The spots of his prime he
  Has rusted with sand ;
Crook-snouted his crest is
  That taper'd so grand.

IX.

How mournful in winter
  The lowing of kine ;
How lean-backed they shiver,
How draggled they cower,
How their nostrils run owre
  With drippings of brine,
So scraggy and crining
  In the cold frost they pine.

* The sides of the cottages plastered with mud or mortar
instead of lime.
† "Chieftain" . . . . salmon.

X,

'Tis hallow-mass time, and
    To mildness farewell !
Its bristles are low'ring
With darkness ; o'erpowering
Are its waters, aye showering
    With onset so fell ;
Seem the kid and the yearling
    As rung their death-knell.

XI.

Every out-lying creature,
    How sinew'd soe'er,
Seeks the refuge of shelter ;
The race of the antler
They snort and they falter,
    A-cold in their lair ;
And the fawns they are wasting
    Since their kin is afar.

XII.

Such the songs that are saddest -
    And dreariest of all ;
I ever am eerie
In the morning to hear ye !
When foddering, to cheer the
    Poor herd in the stall—
While each creature is moaning,
    And sickening in thrall.

Robert Mackay.

FROM "TECUMSEH."

ACT II., SCENE 1.

[Enter Chiefs—The warriors cluster around TECUMSEH, *shouting and discharging their pieces.]*

.   .   .   .   .   .

Tecumseh. Comrades, and faithful warriors of our race !
Ye who defeated Harmar and St. Clair,
And made their hosts a winter's feast for wolves !
I call on you to follow me again,
Not now for war, but as forearmed for flight.
As ever in the past so is it still :
Our sacred treaties are infringed and torn ;
Laughed out of sanctity, and spurned away ;
Used by the Long-Knife's slaves to light the fire,
Or turned to kites by thoughtless boys, whose wrists
Anchor their fathers' lies in front of heaven.
And now we're asked to Council at Vincennes ;
To bend to lawless ravage of our lands,
To treacherous bargains, contracts false, wherein
One side is bound, the other loose as air !
Where are those villains of our race and blood
Who signed those treaties that unseat us here ;
That rob us of rich plains and forests wide ;
And which, consented to, will drive us hence
To stage our lodges in the Northern Lakes,
In penalties of hunger worse than death ?
Where are they ? that we may confront them now
With your wronged sires, your mothers, wives, and
        babes,
And wringing from their false and slavish lips
Confession of their baseness, brand with shame
The traitor hands which sign us to our graves.

Miami Chief. Some are age-bent and blind, and others
     sprawl,
And stagger in the Long-Knife's villages ;
And some are dead, and some have fled away,
And some are lurking in the forest here,
Sneaking, like dogs, until resentment cools.
Kickapoo Chief. We all disclaim their treaties. Should
     they come,
Forced from their lairs by hunger, to our doors,
Swift punishment will light upon their heads.
Tecumseh. Put yokes upon them ! let their mouths be
     bound !
For they are swine who root with champing jaws
Their fathers' fields, and swallow their own offspring.

[*Enter the* PROPHET *in his robe—his face discoloured.*]

The Prophet !
Wecome, my brother, from the lodge of dreams !
Hail to thee, sagest among men—great heir
Of all the wisdom of Pengasega !
Prophet. This pale-face here again ! this hateful snake,
Who crawls between our people and their laws !
Your greeting, brother, takes the chill from mine,
When last we parted you were not so kind.
Tecumseh. The Prophet's wisdom covers all. He
     knows
Why Nature varies in her handiwork,
Moulding one man from snow, the next from fire——
Prophet. Which temper is your own, and blazes up,
In minds of passion like a burning pine.
Tecumseh. 'Twill blaze no more unless to scorch our
     foes.
My brother, there's my hand—for I am grieved
That aught befell to shake our proper love.
Our purpose is too high, and full of danger ;

We have too vast a quarrel on our hands
To waste our breath on this.
                    [*Steps forward and offers his hand.*]
Prophet. My hand to yours.
Several Chiefs. Tecumseh and the Prophet are rejoined !
Tecumseh. Now, but one petty cloud distains our sky.
My brother, this man loves our people well.
                    [*Pointing to Lefroy.*]
Lefroy. I know he hates me, yet I hope to win
My way into his heart.
Prophet.   There—take my hand !
I must dissemble.   Would this palm were poison !
                    [*Aside.*]
[*To Tecumseh.*] What of the Wyandots?   And yet
      I know !
I have been up among the clouds, and down
Into the entrails of the earth, and seen
The dwelling-place of devils.   All my dreams
Are from above, and therefore favour us.
Tecumseh. With one accord the Wyandots disclaim
The treaties of Fort Wayne, and burn with rage.
Their tryst is here, and some will go with me
To Council at Vincennes.   Where's Winnemac?
Miami Chief. That recreant has joined our enemies,
And with the peace-pipe sits beside their fire,
And whiffs away our lives.
Kickapoo Chief.   The Deaf-Chief too,
With head awry, who cannot hear us speak,
Though thunder shouted for us from the skies,
Yet hears the Long-Knives whisper at Vincennes ;
And, when they jest upon our miseries,   [laughter.
Grips his old leathern sides, and coughs with
Delaware Chief. And old Kanaukwa—famed when we
            were young—
Has hid his axe, and washed his honours off.

Tecumseh. 'Tis honor he has parted with, not honors ;
Good deeds are ne'er forespent, nor wiped away.
I know these men ; they've lost their followers,
And, grasping at the shadow of command,
Where sway and custom once had realty,
By times, and turn about, follow each other.
They count for nought—but Winnemac is true,
Though over-politic ; he will not leave us.
Prophet. Those wizened snakes must be destroyed at
    once !
Tecumseh. Have mercy, brother—those poor men are old.
Prophet. Nay, I shall tease them till they sting them-
    selves ;
Their rusty fangs are doubly dangerous.
Tecumseh. What warriors are ready for Vincennes ?
Warriors. All ! All are ready.
Tecumseh leads us on—we follow him.
Tecumseh. Four hundred warriors will go with me,
All armed, yet only for security
Against the deep designs of Harrison.
For 'tis my purpose still to temporise,
Not break with him in war till once again
I scour the far emplacements of our tribes.
Then shall we close at once on all our foes.
They claim our lands, but we shall take their lives ;
Drive out their thievish souls, and spread their bones
To bleach upon the misty Alleghanies ;
Or make death's treaty with them on the spot,
And sign our bloody marks upon their crowns
For lack of schooling—ceding but enough
Of all the lands they covet for their graves.
Miami Chief. Tecumseh's tongue is housed in wisdom's
    cheeks ;
His valour and his prudence march together.
Delaware Chief. 'Tis wise to draw the distant nations on.
This scheme will so extend the Long-Knife force,

In lines defensive stretching to the sea,
Their bands will be but morsels for our braves.
Prophet. How long must this bold project take to ripen?
Time marches with the foe, and his surveyors
Already smudge the forests with their fires.
It frets my blood and makes my bowels turn
To see those devils blaze our ancient oaks,
Cry, " right ! " and drive their rascal pickets down.
Why not make war on them at once ?
Tecumseh.   Not now !
Time will make room for weightier affairs.
Be this the disposition of the hour :
Our warriors from Vincennes will all return,
Save twenty—the companions of my journey—
And this brave white, who longs to share our toil,
And win our love by deeds in our defence.
You, brother, shall remain to guard our town,
Our wives, our children, all that's dear to us—
Receive each fresh accession to our strength ;
And from the hidden world, which you inspect,
Draw a divine instruction for their souls.
Go, now, ye noble chiefs and warriors !
Make preparation—I'll be with you soon.
To-morrow shall we make the Wabash boil,
And beat its current, racing to Vincennes.
          [*Exeunt all but* TECUMSEH *and the* PROPHET.]

.   .   .   .

ACT V., SCENE 2.

A wood near Amherstburg. TECUMSEH's Camp. A vista to
the east—the sun's upper rim just rising above the horizon.

Enter WARRIORS *and* JOSAKEEDS. *The warriors extend their weapons towards the sun. The* JOSAKEEDS
advance facing it.

1st Josakeed. He comes ! Yohewah ! the Great Spirit,
comes
Up from his realm—the place of Breaking Light !
Hush, nations ! Worship, in your souls, the King,
Above all Spirits ! Master of our lives !
I-ge-zis ! He that treads upon the day,
And makes the light !
2nd Josakeed.   He comes ! he comes ! he comes !
The ever-dying, ever-living One !
He hears us, and he speaks thus to mine ears !
I wipe once more the darkness from the earth ;
I look into the forest, and it sings—
The leaves exult ; the waters swim with joy.
I look upon the nations, and their souls
Strengthen with courage to resist their foes.
I will restore them to their father's lands ;
I will pour laughter on the earth, like rain,
And fill the forest with its ancient food.
Corn will be plenteous in the fields as dust,
And fruits, moved to their joy, on every bough
Will glow and gleam like ardent fire and gold.
3rd Josakeed. O, Mighty Spirit ! Guardian of our
Breath !
We see thy body, and yet see thee not.
The spirits in our forms, which no man sees,
Breathe forth to thee, for they are born of thee.
Hear us, thy children, and protect our lives !
Our warriors retreat—it is thy will !
Declare the way—the fateful time to stand !
Then, if in battle they decline in death,
Take them, O Master, to thy Mighty Heart—
Thy Glorious Ground and Shining Place of Souls !
Yohewa ! Master of Breath ! Yohewa ! Hear us!

[*Exeunt.*

Charles Mair.

WITH WALKER IN NICARAGUA.

I.

HE was a brick : let this be said
Above my brave dishonored dead.
I ask no more, this is not much,
Yet I disdain a colder touch
To memory as dear as his :
For he was true as any star,
And brave as Yuba's grizzlies are,
Yet gentle as the panther is
Mouthing her young in her first fierce kiss ;
Tall, courtly, grand as any king,
Yet simple as a child at play,
In camp and court the same alway,
And never moved at anything ;
A dash of sadness in his air,
Born, may be, of his own care,
And, may be, born of a despair
In early love—I never knew ;
I questioned not, as many do,
Of things as sacred as this is ;
I only know that he to me
Was all a father, friend, could be ;
I sought to know no more than this
Of history of him or his.

A piercing eye, a princely air,
A presence like a chevalier,
Half angel and half Lucifer ;
Fair fingers, jewell'd manifold
With great gems set in hoops of gold ;
Sombréro black, with plume of snow
That swept his long silk locks below ;

A red serape with bars of gold,
Heedless, falling, fold on fold ;
A sash of silk, where flashing swung
A sword as swift as serpent's tongue,
In sheath of silver chased in gold ;
A face of blended pride and pain,
Of mingled pleading and disdain,
With shades of glory and of grief ;
And Spanish spurs with bills of steel
That dash'd and dangled at the heel—
The famous filibuster chief
Stood by his tent 'mid tall brown trees
That top the fierce Cordilleras,
With brawn arm arch'd above his brow ;—
Stood still—he stands, a picture, now,—
Long gazing down the sunset seas.

II.

What strange strong bearded men were these
He led toward the tropic seas !
Men sometime of uncommon birth,
Men rich in histories untold,
Who boasted not, though more than bold,
Blown from the four parts of the earth.
Men mighty-thew'd as Samson was,
That had been kings in any cause,
A remnant of the races past ;
Dark-brow'd as if in iron cast,
Broad-breasted as 'twin gates of brass,—
Men strangely brave and fiercely true,
Who dared the West when giants were,
Who err'd, yet bravely dared to err ;
A remnant of that early few
Who held no crime or curse or vice

As dark as that of cowardice ;
With blendings of the worst and best
Of faults and virtues that have blest
Or cursed or thrill'd the human breast.

They rode, a troop of bearded men,
Rode two and two out from the town,
And some were blonde and some were brown,
And all as brave as Sioux ; but when
From San Bennetto south the line
That bound them in the laws of men
Was passed, and peace stood mute behind,
And streamed a banner to the wind
The world knew not, there was a sign
Of awe, of silence, rear and van.
Men thought who never thought before ;
I heard the clang and clash of steel
From sword at hand and spur at heel
And iron feet, but nothing more.
Some thought of Texas, some of Maine,
But more of rugged Tennessee,—
Of scenes in Southern vales of wine,
And scenes in Northern hills of pine,
As scenes they might not meet again ;
And one of Avon thought, and one
Thought of an isle beneath the sun,
And one of Rowley, one the Rhine,
And one turned sadly to the Spree.

Defeat meant something more than death ;
The world was ready, keen to smite,
As stern and still beneath its ban
With iron will and bated breath,
Their hands against their fellow-man,
They rode—each man an Ishmaelite.

But when we struck the hills of pine,
These men dismounted, doffed their cares,
Talked loud and laughed old love affairs,
And on the grass took meat and wine,
And never gave a thought again
To land or life that lay behind,
Or love, or care of any kind
Beyond the present cross or pain.

And I, a waif of stormy seas,
A child among such men as these,
Was blown along this savage surf
And rested with them on the turf,
And took delight below the trees.
I did not question, did not care
To know the right or wrong.   I saw
That savage freedom had a spell,
And loved it more than I can tell,
And snapped my fingers at the law.
I bear my burden of the shame,—
I shun it not, and naught forget,
However much I may regret :
I claim some candour to my name,
And courage cannot change or die.—
Did they deserve to die ? they died.
Let justice then be satisfied,
And as for me, why what am I ?

The standing side by side till death,
The dying for some wounded friend,
The faith that failed not to the end,
The strong endurance till the breath
And body took their ways apart,
I only know, I keep my trust.
Their vices ! earth has them by heart.
Their virtues ! they are with the dust.

How wound we through the solid wood,
With all its broad boughs hung in green,
With lichen-mosses trail'd between !
How waked the spotted beasts of prey,
Deep sleeping from the face of day,
And dash'd them like a troubled flood
Down some defile and denser wood !

And snakes, long, lithe and beautiful
As green and graceful-bough'd bamboo,
Did twist and twine them through and through
The boughs that hung red-fruited full.
One, monster-sized, above me hung,
Close eyed me with his bright pink eyes,
Then raised his folds, and sway'd and swung,

And lick'd like lightning his red tongue,
Then oped his wide mouth with surprise ;
He writhed and curved, and raised and lower'd
His folds like liftings of the tide,
And sank so low I touched his side,
As I rode by, with my broad sword.

The trees shook hands high over head,
And bow'd and intertwined across
The narrow way, while leaves and moss
And luscious fruit, gold-hued and red,
Through all the canopy of green,
Let not one sunshaft shoot between.

Birds hung and swung, green-robed and red,
Or droop'd in curved lines dreamily,
Rainbows reversed, from tree to tree,
Or sang low-hanging overhead—
Sang low, as if they sang and slept,

Sang faint, like some far waterfall,
And took no note of us at all,
Though nuts that in the way were spread
Did crash and crackle as we stept.

Wild lilies, tall as maidens are,
As sweet of breath, as pearly fair,
As fair as faith, as pure as truth,
Fell thick before our every tread,
As in a sacrifice to ruth,
And all the air with perfume fill'd
More sweet than ever man distill'd.
The ripen'd fruit a fragrance shed
And hung in hand-reach overhead,
In nest of blossoms on the shoot,
The bending shoot that bore the fruit.

How ran the monkeys through the leaves !
How rush'd they through, brown clad and blue,
Like shuttles hurried through and through
The threads a hasty weaver weaves !

How quick they cast us fruits of gold,
Then loosen'd hand and all foothold,
And hung limp, limber, as if dead,
Being low and listless overhead ;
And all the time, with half-oped eyes
Bent full on us in mute surprise—
Look'd wisely too, as wise hens do
That watch you with the head askew.

The long days through from blossom'd trees
There came the sweet song of sweet bees,
With chorus-tones of cockatoo
That slid his beak along the bough,

And walk'd and talk'd and hung and swung,
In crown of gold and coat of blue,
The wisest fool that ever sung,
Or had a crown, or had a tongue.

Oh when we broke the sombre wood,
And pierced at last the sunny plain ;
How wild and still with wonder stood
The proud mustangs with banner'd mane,
And necks that never knew a rein,
And nostrils lifted high, and blown,
Fierce breathing as a hurricane :
Yet by their leader held the while
In solid column, square and file,
And ranks more martial than our own !

Some one above the common kind,
Some one to look to, lean upon,
I think is much a woman's mind ;
But it was mine, and I had drawn
A rein beside the chief while we
Rode through the forest leisurely ;
When he grew kind and questioned me
Of kindred, home, and home affair,
Of how I came to wander there,
And had my father herds and land,
And men in hundreds at command ?
At which I silent shook my head,
Then, timid, met his eyes and said,
" Not so.   Where sunny foot-hills ran
Down to the North Pacific sea,
And Williamette meets the sun
In many angles, patiently
My father tends his flocks of snow,
And turns alone the mellow sod
And sows some fields not overbroad,

And mourns my long delay in vain,
Nor bids one serve man come or go ;
While mother from the wheel or churn,
And may be from the milking shed,
There lifts an humble weary head
To watch and wish for my return
Across the camas' blossom'd plain."

He held his bent head very low,
A sudden sadness in his air ;
Then turned and touched my yellow hair
And took the long locks in his hand,
Toyed with them, smiled, and let them go,
Then thrummed about his saddle bow
As thought ran swift across his face ;
Then turning sudden from his place,
He gave some short and quick command.
They brought the best steed of the band,
They hung a bright sword at my side,
They bade me mount and by him ride,
And from that hour to the end
I never felt the need of friend.

Far in the wildest quernine wood
We found a city old—so old,
Its very walls were turn'd to mould,
And stately trees upon them stood.
No history has mentioned it,
No map has given it a place ;
The last dim trace of tribe and race—
The word's forgetfulness is fit.

It held one structure grand and moss'd,
Mighty as any castle sung,
And old when oldest Ind was young,
With threshold Christian never cross'd ;

A temple builded to the sun,
Along whose sombre altar-stone
Brown bleeding virgins had been strown
Like leaves, when leaves are crisp and dun,
In ages ere the sphinx was born,
Or Babylon had birth or morn.

My chief led up the marble step—
He ever led, broad blade in hand—
When down the stones with double hand
Clutch'd to his blade, a savage leapt,
Hot bent to barter life for life.
The chieftain drove his bowie knife
Full through his thick and broad breast-bone,
And broke the point against the stone,
The dark stone of the temple wall.
I saw him loose his hold and fall
Full length with head hung down the step;
I saw run down a ruddy flood
Of rushing pulsing human blood.
Then from the crowd a woman crept
And kissed the gory hands and face,
And smote herself.   Then one by one
The dark crowd crept and did the same,
Then bore the dead man from the place.
Down darken'd aisles the brown priests came,
So picture-like, with sandall'd feet
And long gray dismal grass-wove gowns,
So like the pictures of old time,
And stood all still and dark of frowns,
At blood upon the stones and street.
So we laid ready hands to sword
And boldly spoke some bitter word;
But they were stubborn still, and stood
Dark frowning as a winter wood,
And mutt'ring something of the crime

Of blood upon the temple stone,
As if the first that it had known.

We turned toward the massive door
With clash of steel at heel, and with
Some swords all red and ready drawn.
I traced the sharp edge of my sword
Along the marble wall and floor
For crack or crevice ; there was none.
From one vast mount of marble stone
The mighty temple had been cored
By nut-brown children of the sun,
When stars were newly bright and blithe
Of song along the rim of dawn,
A mighty marble monolith !

.   .   .   .   .   .

III.

Through marches through the mazy wood,
And maybe through too much of blood,
At last we came down to the seas.
A city stood white-wall'd and brown
With age, in nest of orange trees ;
And this we won, and many a town
And rancho reaching up and down,
Then rested in the red-hot days
Beneath the blossom'd orange trees,
Made drowsy with the drum of bees,
And drank in peace the south-sea breeze,
Made sweet with sweeping boughs of bays.

Well ! there were maidens, shy at first,
And then, ere long, not over shy.

Yet pure of soul and proudly chare.
No love on earth has such an eye !
No land there is is bless'd or curs'd
With such a limb or grace of face,
Or gracious form, or genial air !
In all the bleak North-land not one
Hath been so warm of soul to me
As coldest soul by that warm sea,
Beneath the bright hot centred sun.

No lands where any ices are
Approached, or ever dare compare
With warm loves born beneath the sun.
The one the cold white steady star,
The lifted shifting sun the one.
I grant you fond, I grant you fair,
I grant you honor, trust, and truth,
And years as beautiful as youth,
And many years beyond the sun,
And faith as fix'd as any star ;
But all the North-land hath not one
So warm of soul as sun-maids are.

I was but in my boyhood then,
I count my fingers over, so,
And find it years and years ago,
And I am scarcely yet of men.
But I was tall and lithe and fair,
With rippled tide of yellow hair,
And prone to mellowness of heart ;
While she was tawny-red like wine,
With black hair boundless as the night.
As for the rest I knew my part,
At least was apt, and willing quite
To learn, to listen, and incline
To teacher warm and wise like mine.

•   •   •   •   •   •

Let eyes be not dark eyes, but dreams,
Or drifting clouds with flashing fires,
Or far delights, or fierce desires,
Yet not be more than well beseems ;
Let hearts be pure and strong and true,
Let lips be luscious and blood-red,
Let earth in gold be garmented,
And tented in her tent of blue,
Let goodly rivers glide between
Their leaning willow walls of green,
Let all things be fill'd full of sun,
And full of warm winds of the sea,
And I beneath my vine and tree
Take rest, nor war with anyone ;
Then I will thank God with full cause,
Say this is well, is as it was.

•   •   •   •   •   •

Let the unclean think things unclean ;
I swear tip-toed, with lifted hands,
That we were pure as sea-wash'd sands,
That not one coarse thought came between ;
Believe or disbelieve who will,
Unto the pure all things are pure ;
As for the rest, I can endure
Alike the good will or their ill.

She boasted Montezuma's blood,
Was pure of soul as Tahoe's flood,
And strangely fair and princely soul'd,
And she was rich in blood and gold—
More rich in love grown over-bold
From its own consciousness of strength.
How warm !   Oh not for any cause

Could I declare how warm she was,
In her brown beauty and hair's length.
We loved in the sufficient sun,
We lived in elements of fire,
For love is fire and fierce desire ;
Yet lived as pure as priest and nun.

We lay slow rocking in the bay
In birch canoe beneath the crags
Thick, topp'd with palm, like sweeping flags
Between us and the burning day.
The red-eyed crocodile lay low
Or lifted from his rich rank fern,
And watched us and the tide by turn,
And we slow cradled to and fro.

And slow we cradled on till night,
And told the old tale, overtold,
As misers in recounting gold
Each time do take a new delight.
With her pure passion-given grace
She drew her warm self close to me ;
And, her two brown hands on my knee,
And her two black eyes in my face,
She then grew sad and guess'd at ill,
· And in the future seemed to see
With woman's ken of prophecy ;
Yet proffer'd her devotion still.
And plaintive so, she gave a sign,
A token cut of virgin gold,
That all her tribe should ever hold
Its wearer as some one divine,
Nor touch him with a hostile hand.
And I in turn gave her a blade,
A dagger, worn as well by maid
As man, in that half-lawless land ;

It had a massive silver hilt,
Had a most keen and cunning blade,
A gift by chief and comrades made
For reckless blood at Rivas spilt.
" Show this," said I, " too well 'tis known,
And worth a hundred lifted spears,
Should ill beset your sunny years ;
There is not one in Walker's band,
But at the sight of this alone,
Will reach a brave and ready hand,
And make your right or wrong his own."

IV.

.   •   •   •   •   '

Ill comes disguised in many forms ;
Fair winds are but a prophecy
Of foulest winds full soon to be—
The brighter these, the blacker they ;
The clearest night has darkest day,
And brightest days bring blackest storms.
There came reverses to our arms ;
I saw the signal-light's alarms
At night red crescenting the bay.
The foe poured down a flood next day
As strong as tides when tides are high,
And drove us bleeding to the sea,
In such wild haste of flight that we
Had hardly time to arm and fly.

Blown from the shore, borne far a-sea,
I lifted my two hands on high
With wild soul splashing to the sky,
And cried, " O more than crowns to me,
Farewell at last to love and thee ! "
I walked the deck, I kissed my hand

Back to the far and fading shore,
And bent a knee as to implore,
Until the last dark head of land
Slid down behind the dimpled sea.
At last I sank in troubled sleep,
A very child, rock'd by the deep,
Sad questioning the fate of her
Before the savage conqueror.

The loss of comrades, power, place,
A city wall'd, cool shaded ways,
Cost me no care at all ; somehow
I only saw her sad brown face,
And—I was younger then than now.

Red flash'd the sun across the deck,
Slow flapp'd the idle sails, and slow
The black ship cradled to and fro.
Afar my city lay, a speck
Of white against a line of blue ;
Around, half-lounging on the deck,
Some comrades chatted two by two.
I held a new-fill'd glass of wine,
And with the mate talk'd as in play
· Of fierce events of yesterday,
To coax his light life into mine.

He jerk'd the wheel, as slow he said,
· Low laughing with averted head,
And so, half sad : " You bet they'll fight ;
They followed in canim, canoe,
A perfect fleet, that on the blue,
Lay dancing till the mid of night.
Would you believe ! one little cuss—
(He turned his stout head slow sidewise,
And 'neath his hat-rim took the skies)—

In petticoats did follow us
The livelong night, and at the dawn
Her boat lay rocking in the lee,
Scarce one short pistol-shot from me."
This said the mate, half mournfully,
Then peck'd at us ; for he had drawn,
By bright light heart and homely wit,
A knot of us around the wheel,
Which he stood whirling like a reel,
For still the ship reck'd not of it.

" And where's she now ? " one careless said,
With eyes slow lifting to the brine,
Swift swept the instant far by mine ;
The bronzed mate listed, shook his head,
Spirted a stream of amber wide
Across and over the ship side,
Jerk'd at the wheel and slow replied :

" She had a dagger in her hand,
She rose, she raised it, tried to stand,
But fell, and so upset herself :
Yet still the poor brown savage elf,
Each time the long light wave would toss
And lift her form from out the sea,
Would shake a strange bright blade at me,
With rich hilt chased a cunning cross.
At last she sank, but still the same
She shook the dagger in the air,
As if to still defy and dare,
And sinking seem'd to call your name."

I dash'd my wine against the wall,
I rush'd across the deck, and all
The sea I swept and swept again,
With lifted hand, with eye and glass,

But all was idle and in vain.
I saw a red-bill'd sea-gull pass,
A petrel sweeping round and round,
I heard the far white sea-surf sound,
But no sign could I hear or see
Of one so more than seas to me.

I cursed the ship, the shore, the sea,
The brave brown mate, the bearded men ;
I had a fever then, and then
Ship, shore, and sea were one to me ;
And weeks we on the dead waves lay,
And I more truly dead than they.
At last some rested on an isle ;
The few strong-breasted with a smile
Returning to the sunny shore,
Scarce counting of the pain and cost,
Scarce recking if they won or lost ;
They sought but action, ask'd no more ;
They counted life but as a game,
With full per cent. against them, and
Staked all upon a single hand,
And lost or won, content the same.

I never saw my chief again,
I never sought again the shore,
Or saw my white-wall'd city more.
I could not bear the more than pain
At sight of blossom'd orange trees
Or blended song of birds and bees,
The sweeping shadows of the palm
Or spicy breath of bay or balm.
And striving to forget the while,
I wander'd through the dreary isle,
Here black with juniper, and there
Made white with goats in summer coats,

The only things that anywhere
We found with life in all the land,
Save birds that ran, long-bill'd and brown,
Long-legg'd and still as shadows are,
Like dancing shadows up and down
The sea-rim on the swelt'ring sand.

The warm sea laid his dimpled face,
With every white hair smoothed in place,
As if asleep against the land ;
Great turtles slept upon his breast,
As thick as eggs in any nest ;
I could have touched them with my hand.

   .   .   .   .   .

The days and grass grew long together ;
They now fell short and crisp again,
And all the fair face of the main
Grew dark and wrinkled at the weather.
Through all the summer sun's decline
Fell news of triumphs and defeats,
Of hard advances, hot retreats—
Then days and days and not a line.

At last one night they came. I knew
Ere yet the boat had touched the land
That all were lost : they were so few,
I near could count them on one hand ;
But he, the leader, led no more.
The proud chief still disdain'd to fly,
But, like one wreck'd, clung to the shore,
And struggled on, and struggling fell
From power to a prison-cell,
And only left that cell to die.

   .   .   .   .   .

My recollection, like a ghost,
Goes from this sea to that sea-side,
Goes and returns as turns the tide,
Then turns again unto the coast.
I know not which I mourn the most,
My brother or my virgin bride,
My chief or my unwedded wife.
The one was as the lordly sun,
To joy in, bask in, and admire ;
The peaceful moon was as the one,
To love, to look to, and desire ;
And both a part of my young life.

.   .   .   .   ,

Years after, shelter'd from the sun
Beneath a Sacramento bay,
A black Muctacto by me lay
Along the long grass crisp and dun,
His brown mule browsing by his side,
And told with all a Peon's pride,
How he once fought, how long and well,
Broad breast to breast, red hand to hand,
Against a foe for his fair land,
And how the fierce invader fell ;
And artless told me how he died.

To die with hands and brow unbound
He gave his gems and jewell'd sword ;
Thus at the last the warrior found
Some freedom for his steel's reward.
He walk'd out from the prison-wall
Dress'd like a prince for a parade,
And made no note of man or maid,
But gazed out calmly over all ;

Then look'd afar, half paused, and then
Above the mottled sea of men
He kissed his thin hand to the sun ;
Then smiled so proudly none had known
But he was stepping to a throne,
Yet took no note of any one.
A nude brown beggar Peon child,
Encouraged as the captive smiled,
Look'd up half scared, half pitying ;
He stoop'd, he caught it from the sands,
Put bright coins in its two brown hands,
Then strode on like another king.

Two deep, a musket's length, they stood,
A-front, in sandals, nude, and dun
As death and darkness wove in one,
Their thick lips thirsting for his blood.
He took their black hands one by one,
And, smiling with a patient grace,
Forgave them all and took his place.
He bared his broad brow to the sun,
Gave one long last look to the sky,
The white-wing'd clouds that hurried by,
The olive hills in orange hue ;
A last list to the cockatoo
That hung by beak from cocoa-bough
Hard by, and hung and sung as though
He never was to sing again,
Hung all red-crown'd and robed in green,
With belts of gold and blue between.—

A bow, a touch of heart, a fall
Of purple smoke, a crash, a thud,
A warrior's raiment rent, and blood,
A face in dust, and—that was all.

Success had made him more than king;
Defeat made him the vilest thing
In name, contempt, or hate can bring;
So much the leaded dice of war
Do make or mar of character.

Speak ill who will of him, he died
In all disgrace; say of the dead
His heart was black, his hands were red—
Say this much, and be satisfied:
Gloat over it all undenied.
I only say that he to me,
Whatever he to others was,
Was truer far than anyone
That I have known beneath the sun,
Sinner, or saint, or Pharisee,
As boy or man, for any cause;
I only say he was my friend
When strong of hand and fair of fame;
Dead and disgraced, I stand the same
To him, and so shall to the end.

I lay this crude wreath on his dust;
Inwove with sad, sweet memories
Recall'd here by the colder seas.
I leave the wild bird with his trust,
To sing and say him nothing wrong;
I wake no rivalry of song.

He lies low in the levell'd sand,
Unshelter'd from the tropic sun,
And now of all he·knew not one
Will speak him fair in that far land.

Perhaps 'twas this that made me seek,
Disguised, his grave one winter-tide ;
A weakness for the weaker side,
A siding with the helpless weak.

A palm not far held out a hand,
Hard by a long green bamboo swung,
And bent like some great bow unstrung,
And quiver'd like a willow wand ;
Beneath a broad banana's leaf,
Perch'd on its fruits that crooked hang,
A bird in rainbow splendour sang
A low sad song of temper'd grief.

No sod, no sign, no cross nor stone,
But at his side a cactus green
Upheld its lances long and keen ;
It stood in hot red sands alone,
Flat palm'd and fierce with lifted spears ;
One bloom of crimson crowned its head,
A drop of blood so bright—so red ;
Yet redolent as roses tears.

In my left hand I held a shell,
All rosy lipp'd and pearly red ;
I laid it by his lowly bed,
For he did love so passing well
The grand songs of the solemn sea.
O shell ! sing well, wild, with a will,
When storms blow loud and birds be still,
The wildest sea-song known to thee !

I said some things, with folded hands,
Soft whisper'd in the dim sea-sound,
And eyes held humbly to the ground,
And frail knees sunken in the sands.

He had done more than this for me,
And yet I could not well do more :
I turned me down the olive shore,
And set a sad face to the sea.

Joaquin Miller.

KIT CARSON'S RIDE.

" RUN ?   Now you bet you ; I rather guess so !
But he's blind as a badger.   Whoa, Paché, boy, whoa.
No, you wouldn't believe it to look at his eyes,
But he is, badger blind, and it happened this wise.

" We lay in the grasses and the sun-burnt clover
That spread on the ground like a great brown cover
Northward and southward, and west and away
To the Brazos, to where our lodges lay,
One broad and unbroken sea of brown,
Awaiting the curtains of night to come down
To cover us over and conceal our flight
With my brown bride, won from an Indian town
That lay in the rear the full ride of a night.

" We lounged in the grasses—her eyes were in mine,
And her hands on my knee, and her hair was as wine
In its wealth and its flood, pouring on and all over
Her bosom wine-red, and pressed never by one ;
And her touch was as warm as the tinge of the clover
Burnt brown as it reached to the kiss of the sun,
And her words were as low as the lute-throated dove,
And as laden with love as the heart when it beats
In its hot eager answer to earliest love,
Or the bee hurried home by its burthen of sweets.

"We lay low in the grass on the broad plain levels,
Old Revels and I, and my stolen brown bride ;
And the heavens of blue and the harvest of brown
And beautiful clover were welded as one,
To the right and the left, in the light of the sun.
'Forty full miles if a foot to ride,
Forty full miles if a foot, and the devils
Of red Comanches are hot on the track
When once they strike it.   Let the sun go down
Soon, very soon,' muttered bearded old Revels,
As he peered at the sun, lying low on his back,
Holding fast to his lasso.   Then he jerked at his steed
And he sprang to his feet, and glanced swiftly around,
And then dropped as if shot, with his ear to the ground :
Then again to his feet, and to me, to my bride,
While his eyes were like fire, his face like a shroud,
His form like a king and his beard like a cloud,
And his voice loud and shrill, as if blown from a reed,—
'Pull, pull in your lassos, and bridle to steed,
And speed you if ever for life you would speed,
And ride for your lives, for your lives you must ride !
For the plain is aflame, and the prairie on fire,
And the feet of wild horses hard flying before
I hear, like a sea breaking high on the shore,
While the buffalo come like a surge of the sea,
Driven far by the flame, driving fast on us three,
As a hurricane comes, crushing palms in his ire.'

"We drew in the lassos, seized saddle and rein,
Threw them on, switched them on, switched them over
   again,
And again drew the girth, cast aside the masheers,
Cut away tapidaros, loosed the sash from its fold,
Cast aside the catenas red-spangled with gold,
And gold-mounted Colts, the companions of years,
Cast the silken serapes to the wind in a breath,

And so bared to the skin sprang all haste to the horse—
As bare as when born, as when new from the hand
Of God—without word ; or one word of command.
Turned head to the Brazos in a red race with death,
Turned head to the Brazos with a breath in the air
Blowing hot from a king leaving death in his course ;
Turned head to the Brazos with a sound in the air
Like the rush of an army, and a flash in the eye
Of a red wall of fire reaching up to the sky,
Stretching fierce in pursuit of a black rolling sea
Rushing fast upon us, as the wind, sweeping free
And afar from the desert, blew hollow and hoarse.

"Not a word, not a wail from a lip was let fall,
Not a kiss from my bride, not a look nor low call
Of love-note or courage ; but on o'er the plain
So steady and still, leaning low to the mane,
With the heel to the flank and the hand to the rein,
Rode we on, rode we three, rode we nose to gray nose,
Reaching long, breathing loud, as a creviced wind blows ;
Yet we broke not a whisper, we breathed not a prayer,
There was work to be done, there was death in the air,
And the chance was as one to a thousand for all.

"Gray nose to gray nose, and each steady mustang
Stretched neck and stretched nerve till the arid earth
    rang,
And the foam from the flank and the croup and the neck
Flew around like the spray on a storm-driven deck.
Twenty miles ! . . . thirty miles ! . . . a dim distant
    speck . . .
Then a long-reaching line, and the Brazos in sight,
And I rose in my seat with a shout of delight.
I stood in my stirrup and looked to my right—
But Revels was gone ; I glanced by my shoulder
And saw his horse stagger ; I saw his head drooping

Hard down on his breast, and his naked breast stooping
Low down to the mane, as so swifter and bolder
Ran reaching out for us the red-footed fire.
To right and to left the black buffalo came,
A terrible surf on a red sea of flame
Rushing on in the rear, reaching high, reaching higher.
And he rode neck to neck to a buffalo bull,
The monarch of millions, with shaggy mane full
Of smoke and of dust, and it shook with desire
Of battle, with rage and with bellowings loud
And unearthly, and up through its lowering cloud
Came the flash of his eyes like a half-hidden fire,
While his keen crooked horns, through the storm of his
    mane,
Like black lances lifted and lifted again ;
And I looked but this once, for the fire licked through,
And he fell and was lost, as we rode two and two.

 "I looked to my left then—and nose, neck, and
    shoulder
Sank slowly, sank surely, till back to my thighs ;
And up through the black blowing veil of her hair
Did beam full in mine her two marvellous eyes,
With a longing and love, yet a look of despair
And of pity for me as she felt the smoke fold her,
And flames reaching far for her glorious hair.
Her sinking steed faltered, his eager ears fell
To and fro and unsteady, and all the neck's swell
Did subside and recede, and the nerves fell as dead.
Then she saw sturdy Paché still lorded his head,
With a look of delight ; for nor courage nor bribe,
Nor aught but my bride, could have brought him to me.
For he was her father's, and at South Santafee
Had once won a whole herd, sweeping every thing down
In a race where the world came to run for the crown.
And so when I won the true heart of my bride—

My neighbour's and deadliest enemy's child,
And child of the kingly war-chief of his tribe—
She brought me this steed to the border the night
She met Revels and me in her perilous flight
From the lodge of the chief to the North Brazos side ;
And said, so half guessing of ill as she smiled,
As if.jesting, that I, and I only, should ride
The fleet-footed Paché, so if kin should pursue
I should surely escape without other ado
Than to ride, without blood, to the North Brazos side,
And await her—and wait till the next hollow moon
Hung her horn in the palms, when surely and soon
And swift she would join me, and all would be well
Without bloodshed or word.   And now as she fell
From the front, and went down in the ocean of fire,
The last that I saw was a look of delight
That I should escape—a love—a desire—
Yet never a word, not one look of appeal,
Lest I should reach hand, should stay hand or stay heel
One instant for her in my terrible flight.

" Then the rushing of fire around me and under,
And the howling of beasts and a sound as of thunder—
Beasts burning and blind and forced onward and over,
As the passionate flame reached around them and wove her
Red hands in their hair, and kissed hot till they died—
Till they died with a wild and desolate moan,
As a sea heart-broken on the hard brown stone. . . .
And into the Brazos . . . I rode all alone—
All alone, save only a horse long-limbed,
And blind and bare and burnt to the skin.
Then just as the terrible sea came in
And tumbled its thousands hot into the tide,
Till the tide blocked up and the swift stream brimmed
In eddies, we struck on the opposite side.

DEAD IN THE SIERRAS. III

"Sell Paché—blind Paché? now Mister, look here,
You have slept in my tent and partook of my cheer
Many days, many days on this rugged frontier,
For the ways they were rough and Comanches were
     near ;
But you'd better pack up, sir ! This tent is too small
For us two after that ! Has an old mountaineer,
Do you book-men believe, got no tum-tum at all?
Sell Paché ! You buy him ! A bag full of gold !
You show him ! Tell of him the tale I have told !
Why, he bore me through fire, and is blind and is old !
. . . Now pack up your papers, and get up and spin
To them cities you tell of . . Blast you and your tin !"

                                    Joaquin Miller.

DEAD IN THE SIERRAS.

His footprints have failed us,
   Where berries are red,
And madronas are rankest.
   The hunter is dead !

The grizzly may pass
   By his half-open door ;
May pass and repass
   On his path as of yore ;

The panther may crouch
   In the leaves on his limb ;
May scream and may scream—
   It is nothing to him.

Prone, bearded, and breasted
　Like columns of stone ;
And tall as a pine—
　As a pine overthrown !

His camp-fire's gone,
　What else can be done
Than let him sleep on
　Till the light of the sun ?

Ay, tombless ! what of it ?
　Marble is dust,
Cold and repellent ;
　And iron is rust.

Joaquin Miller.

AFTER THE BOAR HUNT.

I.

'TWERE better blow trumpets 'gainst love, keep away
That traitorous urchin with fire or shower,
Or fair or foul means you may have in your power,
Than have him come near you for one little hour.
Take physic, consult with your doctor, as you
Would fight a contagion ; carry all through
The populous day some drug that smells loud,
As you pass on your way, or make way through the
　crowd.
Talk war, or carouse ; only keep off the day
Of his coming, with every true means in your way.

II.

Blow smoke in the eyes of the world, and laugh
With the broad-chested men, as you loaf at your inn,
As you crowd to your inn from your saddles and quaff
The red wine from a horn ; while your dogs at your feet,
Your slim spotted dogs, like the fawn, and as fleet,
Crouch patiently by and look up at your face,
As they wait for the call of the horn to the chase :
For you shall not suffer, and you shall not sin,
Until peace goes out, and till love comes in.

III.

Love horses and hounds, meet many good men—
Yea, men are most proper, and keep you from care.
There is strength in a horse.   There is pride in his will :
It is sweet to look back as you climb the steep hill.
There is room.   You have movement of limb ; you have
    air,
Have the smell of the wood, of the grasses ; and then
What comfort to rest, as you lie thrown at length
All night and alone, with your fists full of strength.

Joaqu.n Miller.

FROM " ARIZONIAN."

, ...

HIS brow was brown'd by the sun and weather,
And touched by the terrible hand of time ;
His rich black beard had a fringe of rime,
As silk and silver inwove together.
There were hoops of gold all over his hands,
And across his breast, in chains and bands,
Broad and massive as belts of leather.

And the belts of gold were bright in the sun,
But brighter than gold his black eyes shone
From their sad face-setting so swarth and dun,
Brighter than beautiful Santan stone,
Brighter even than balls of fire,
As he said, hot-faced, in the face of the Squire :—

" The pines bow'd over, the stream bent under
The cabin cover'd with thatches of palm,
Down in a cañon so deep, the wonder
Was what it could know in its clime but calm.
Down in a cañon so cleft asunder
By sabre-stroke in the young world's prime,
It look'd as broken by bolts of thunder,
And bursted asunder and rent and riven
By earthquakes driven, the turbulent time
A red cross lifted red hands to heaven.
And this in the land where the sun goes down,
And gold is gather'd by tide and by stream,
And maidens are brown as the cocoa brown,
And a life is a love and a love is a dream ;
Where the winds come in from the far Cathay
With odour of spices and balm and bay,
And summer abideth for aye and aye,
Nor comes in a tour with the stately June,
And comes too late and returns too soon
To the land of the sun and of summer's noon.

" She stood in the shadows as the sun went down,
Fretting her curls with her fingers brown,
As tall as the silk-tipp'd tassel'd corn—
Stood strangely watching as I weigh'd the gold,
We had wash'd that day where the river roll'd ;
And her proud lip curl'd with a sun-clime scorn,
As she ask'd, ' Is she better or fairer than I ?—
She, that blonde in the land beyond,

Where the sun is hid and the seas are high—
That you gather in gold as the years go on,
And hoard and hide it away for her
As a squirrel burrows the black pine-burr ?'

"Now the gold weigh'd well, but was lighter of
    weight
Than we two had taken for days of late,
So I was fretted, and, brow a-frown,
I said, ' She is fairer, and I loved her first,
And shall love her last come the worst to worst.'
Now her eyes were black and her skin was brown,
But her lips grew livid and her eyes a-fire
As I said this thing : and higher and higher
The hot words ran, when the booming thunder
Peal'd in the crags and the pine-tops under,
While up by the cliff in the murky skies
It look d as the clouds had caught the fire—
The flash and fire of her wonderful eyes.

"She turn'd from the door and down to the river,
And mirror'd her face in the whimsical tide ;
Then threw back her hair as if throwing a quiver,
As an Indian throws it back from his side
And free from his hands, swinging fast to the shoulder
When rushing to battle ; and, rising, she sigh'd
And shook and shiver'd as aspens shiver.
Then a great green snake slid into the river,
Glistening, green, and with eyes of fire ;
Quick, double-handed, she seized a boulder,
And cast it with all the fury of passion,
As with lifted head it went curving across,
Swift darting its tongue like a fierce desire,
Curving and curving, lifting higher and higher,
Bent and beautiful as a river moss ;
Then, smitten, it turn'd, bent, broken and doubled,

And lick'd, red-tongued, like a forkèd fire,
And sank, and the troubled waters bubbled,
And then swept on in their old swift fashion.

" I lay in my hammock : the air was heavy
And hot and threat'ning ; the very heaven
Was holding its breath ; and bees in a bevy
Hid under my thatch ; and birds were driven
In clouds to the rocks in a hurried whirr
As I passed down by the path for her.
She stood like a bronze bent over the river,
The proud eyes fix'd, the passion unspoken,—
When the heavens broke like a great dyke broken.
Then, ere I fairly had time to give her
A shout of warning, a rushing of wind,
And the rolling of clouds, and a deafening din,
And a darkness that had been black to the blind
Came down, as I shouted, ' Come in !   Come in !
Come under the roof, come up from the river,
As up from a gra ve—come now, or come never ! '
The tassel'd tops of the pines were as weeds,
The red-woods rocked like to lake-side reeds,
And the world seemed darkened and drowned for ever.

"One time in the night as the black wind shifted,
And a flash of lightning stretched over the stream,
I seemed to see her with her brown hands lifted—
Only seemed to see, as one sees in a dream—
With her eyes wide, wild, and her pale lips press'd,
And the blood from her brow and the flood to her
        breast ;
When the flood caught her hair as the flax in a wheel,
And wheeling and whirling her round like a reel,
Laugh'd loud her despair, then leapt long like a steed,
Holding tight to her hair, folding fast to her heel,
Laughing fierce, leaping far as if spurr'd to its speed. . .

Now mind, I tell you all this did but seem—
Was seen as you see fearful scenes in a dream ;
For what the devil could the lightning show
In a night like that, I should like to know !

" And then I slept, and sleeping I dreamed
Of great green serpents with tongues of fire,
And of death by drowning, and of after death—
Of the Day of Judgment, wherein it seemed
That she, the heathen, was bidden higher,
Higher than I, that I clung to her side,
And clinging, struggled, and struggling cried,
And crying wakened, all weak of my breath.

" Long leaves of the sun lay over the floor,
And a chipmonk chirped in the open door,
But above on the crag the eagle scream'd,
Scream'd as he never had scream'd before.
I rush'd to the river : the flood had gone
Like a thief, with only his tracks upon
The weeds and grasses and warm wet sand ;
And I ran after with reaching hand,
And call'd as I reach'd and reach'd as I ran,
And ran till I came to the cañon's van,
Where the waters lay in a bent lagoon,
Hook'd and crook'd like the hornèd moon.

" Here in the surge where the waters met,
And the warm wave lifted, and the winds did fret
The wave till it foam'd with rage on the land,
She lay with the wave on the warm white sand ;
Her rich hair trail'd with the trailing weeds,
And her small brown hands lay prone or lifted
As the wave sang strophes in the broken reeds,
Or paused in pity, and in silence sifted
Sands of gold, as upon her grave.

And as sure as you see yon browsing kine,
And breathe the breath of your meadows fine,
When I went to my waist in the warm white wave
And stood all pale in the wave to my breast,
And reach'd for her in her rest and unrest,
Her hands were lifted and reach'd to mine.

"Now mind, I tell you I cried, 'Come in!
Come in to the house, come out from the hollow,
Come out of the storm, come up from the river!'
Cried, and call'd, in that desolate din,
Though I did not rush out and in plain words give her
A wordy warning of the flood to follow,
Word by word and letter by letter:
But she knew it as well as I, and better;
For once in the desert of New Mexico,
When I sought frantically far and wide
For the famous spot where Apaches shot
With bullets of gold their buffalo,
And she followed faithfully at my side,
I threw me down in the hard hot sand
Utterly famish'd, and ready to die,
And a speck arose in the red-hot sky—
A speck no larger than a lady's hand—
While she at my side bent tenderly over,
Shielding my face from the sun as a cover,
And wetting my face, as she watched by my side,
From a skin she had borne till the high noon-tide,
(I had emptied mine in the heat of the morning)
When the thunder muttered far over the plain
Like a monster bound or a beast in pain,
She sprang the instant and gave the warning,
With her brown hand pointed to the burning skies.
I was too weak unto death to arise,
And I prayed for death in my deep despair,
And did curse and clutch in the sand in my rage,

And bite in the bitter white ashen sage,
That covers the desert like a coat of hair ;
But she knew the peril, and her iron will,
With heart as true as the great North Star,
Did bear me up to the palm-tipped hill,
Where the fiercest beasts in a brotherhood,
Beasts that had fled from the plain and far,
In perfected peace expectant stood,
With their heads held high and their limbs a-quiver,
And ere she barely had time to breathe
The boiling waters began to seethe
From hill to hill in a booming river,
Beating and breaking from hill to hill—
Even while yet the sun shot fire,
Without the shield of a cloud above—
Filling the cañon as you would fill
A wine-cup, drinking in swift desire,
With the brim new-kiss'd by the lips you love.

" So you see she knew,—knew perfectly well,
As well as I could shout and tell,
The mountains would send a flood to the plain,
Sweeping the gorge like a hurricane,
When the fire flash'd, and the thunder fell.
Therefore it is wrong, and I say therefore
Unfair, that a mystical brown-wing'd moth
Or midnight bat should for evermore
Fan my face with its wings of air,
And follow me up, down, everywhere,
Flit past, pursue me, or fly before,
Dimly limning in each fair place
The full fix'd eyes and the sad brown face,
So forty times worse than if it were wroth."

Joaquin Miller.

FROM "THE LAST TASCHASTAS."

.　　.　　.　　.　　.　　.

From cold east shore to warm west sea
The red men follow'd the red sun,
And, faint and failing fast as he,
Felt, sure as his, their race was run.
This ancient tribe, press'd to the wave,
There fain had slept a patient slave,
And died out as red embers die
From flames that once leapt hot and high ;
But, roused to anger, half arose
Around that chief a sudden flood,
A hot and hungry cry for blood ;
Half drowsy shook a feeble hand,
Then sank back in a tame repose,
And left him to his fate and foes,
A stately wreck upon the strand.

His was no common mould of mind,
But made for action, ill or good,
Cast in another land and scene
His restless, reckless will had been
A curse or blessing to his kind. -
His eye was like the lightning's wing,
His voice was like a rushing flood ;
He boasted Montyuma's blood,
And when a captive bound he stood
His presence look'd the perfect king.

'Twas held at first that he should die :
I never knew the reason why
A milder counsel did prevail,
Save that we shrank from blood, and save
That brave men do respect the brave.

Down sea sometimes there was a sail,
And far at sea, they said, an isle,
And he was sentenced to exile,
In open boat upon the sea
To go the instant on the main,
And never under penalty
Of death, to touch the shore again.
A troop of bearded buck-skinned men
Bore him hard-hurried to the wave,
Placed him swift in the boat ; and when
Swift pushing to the bristled sea,
His daughter rushed down suddenly,
Threw him his bow, leaped from the shore
Into the boat beside the brave,
And sat her down, and seized the oar,
And never questioned, made replies,
Or moved her lips, or raised her eyes.

His breast was like a gate of brass,
His brow was like a gather'd storm ;
There is no chisell'd stone that has
So stately and complete a form,
In sinew, arm, and every part,
In all the galleries of art.

Gray, bronzed, and naked to the waist,
He stood half halting in the prow,
With quiver bare and idle bow.
His daughter sat with her sad face
Bent on the wave, with her two hands
Held tightly to the dripping oar ;
And as she sat her dimpled knee
Bent lithe as wand of willow tree,
So round and full, so rich and free,
That no one would have ever known
That it had either joint or bone.

The warm sea fondled with the shore,
And laid his white face on the sands.

Her eyes were black, her face was brown,
Her breasts were bare, and there fell down
Such wealth of hair, it almost hid
The two, in its rich jetty fold—
Which I had sometime fain forbid,
They were so richer, fuller far
Than any polish'd bronzes are,
And richer hued than any gold.
On her brown arms, and her brown hands
Were hoops of gold and golden bands,
Rough hammer'd from the virgin ore,
So heavy, they could hold no more.

I wonder now, I wondered then,
That men who fear'd not gods nor men
Laid no rude hand at all on her.
I think she had a dagger slid
Down in her silver'd wampum belt,
It might have been, instead of hilt,
A flashing diamond hurry-hid
That I beheld—I could not know
For certain, we did hasten so ;
And I know now less sure than then.
Deeds strangle memories of deeds,
Red blossoms wither, choked with weeds,
And floods drown memories of men.
Some things have happened since,—and then
This happened years and years ago.

"Go, go ! " the captain cried, and smote
With sword and boot the swaying boat,
Until it quiver'd as at sea
And brought the old chief to his knee.

He turn'd his face, and turning rose
With hand raised fiercely to his foes :
"Yes, we will go, last of my race,
Push'd by the robbers ruthlessly
Into the hollows of the sea,
From this the last, last resting-place.
Traditions of my Fathers say
A feeble few reach'd for the land,
And we reach'd them a welcome hand,
Of old, upon another shore ;
Now they are strong, we weak as they,
And they have driven us before
Their faces, from that sea to this :
Then marvel not if we have sped
Sometimes an arrow as we fled,
So keener than a serpent's hiss."

He turn'd a time unto the sun
That lay half hidden in the sea,
As in his hollows rocked asleep,
All trembled and breathed heavily ;
Then arch'd his arm as you have done,
For sharp masts piercing through the deep.
No shore or tall ship met the eye,
Or isle, or sail, or anything,
Save white sea-gulls on dripping wing,
And mobile sea and molten sky.

"Farewell !—push seaward, child !" he cried,
And quick the paddle-strokes replied.
Like lightning from the panther-skin
That bound his loins round about
He snatched a poison'd arrow out,
That like a snake lay hid within,
And twanged his bow.   The captain fell
Prone on his face, and such a yell

GOLU.

Of triumph from that savage rose
As man may never hear again.
He stood as standing on the main,
The topmost main, in proud repose,
And shook his clench'd fist at his foes,
And called, and cursed them every one.
He heeded not the shouts and shot
That follow'd him, but grand and grim
Stood up against the level sun ;
And standing so, seem'd in his ire
So grander than a leaping fire.

And when the sun had left the sea,
That laves Abrip, that Blanco laves,
And left the land to death and me,
The only thing that I could see
Was, even as the light boat lay
High lifted on the white-backed waves,
A head as grey and tossed as they.

Joaquin Miller.

GOLU.

ONCE I had a little sweetheart
In the land of the Malay,—
Such a little yellow sweetheart !
Warm and peerless as the day
Of her own dear sunny island,
Keimah, in the far, far East,
Where the mango and banana
Made us many a merry feast.

Such a little copper sweetheart
Was my Golu, plump and round,

GOLU.

With her hair all blue-black streaming
O'er her to the very ground.
Soft and clear as dew-drop clinging
To a grass blade was her eye ;
For the heart below was purer
Than the hill-stream whispering by.

Costly robes were not for Golu :
No more raiment did she need
Than the milky budding breadfruit,
Or the lily of the mead ;
And she was my little sweetheart
Many a sunny summer day,
When we ate the fragrant guavas,
In the land of the Malay.

Life was laughing then.   Oh ! Golu,
Do you think of that old time,
And of all the tales I told you
Of my colder Western clime?
Do you think how happy were we
When we sailed to strip the palm,
And we made a latten arbor
Of the boat-sail in the calm ?

They may call you semi-savage,
Golu ! I cannot forget
How I poised my little sweetheart
Like a copper statuette.
Now my path lies through the cities ;
But they cannot drive away
My sweet dreams of little Golu
And the land of the Malay.

John Boyle O' Reilly.

THE DUKITE SNAKE.

A WEST AUSTRALIAN BUSHMAN'S STORY.

WELL, mate, you've asked me about a fellow
You met to-day, in a black-and-yellow
Chain-gang suit, with a pedlar's pack,
Or some such burden, strapped to his back.
Did you meet him square? No, passed you by?
Well, if you had, and had looked in his eye,
You'd have felt for your irons then and there;
For the light in his eye is the madman's glare.
Ay, mad, poor fellow! I know him well,
And if you're not sleepy just yet, I'll tell
His story,—a strange one as ever you heard
Or read; but I'll vouch for it, every word.

You just wait a minute, mate: I must see
How that damper's doing, and make some tea.
You smoke? That's good; for there's plenty of weed
In that wallaby skin. Does your horse feed
In the hobbles? Well he's got good feed here,
And my own old bush mare won't interfere.
Done with that meat? Throw it there to the dogs,
And fling on a couple of banksia logs.

And now for the story. That man who goes
Through the bush with the pack and the convict's
    clothes
Has been mad for years; but he does no harm,
And our lonely settlers feel no alarm
When they see or meet him. Poor Dave Sloane
Was a settler once, and a friend of my own.
Some eight years back, in the spring of the year,
Dave came from Scotland, and settled here.

THE DUKITE SNAKE. 127

A splendid young fellow he was just then,
And one of the bravest and truest men
That I ever met : he was kind as a woman
To all who needed a friend, and no man—
Not even a convict—met with his scorn,
For David Sloane was a gentleman born.
Ay, friend, a gentleman, though it sounds queer:
There's plenty of blue blood flowing out here,
And some younger sons of your "upper ten"
Can be met with here, first-rate bushmen.
Why, friend, I ——
                    Bah ! curse that dog ! you see
This talking so much has affected me.

Well, Sloane came here with an axe and a gun ;
He bought four miles of a sandal-wood run.
This bush at that time was a lonesome place,
So lonesome the sight of a white man's face
Was a blessing, unless it came at night,
And peered in your hut, with the cunning fright
Of a runaway convict ; and even they
Were welcome, for talk's sake, while they could stay.
Dave lived with me here for a while, and learned
The tricks of the bush,—how the snare was laid
In the wallaby track, how traps were made,
How 'possums and kangaroo rats were killed ;
And when that was learned, I helped him to build
From mahogany slabs a good bush hut,
And showed him how sandal-wood logs were cut.
I lived up there with him days and days,
For I loved the lad for his honest ways.
I had only one fault to find : at first
Dave worked too hard ; for a lad who was nursed,
As he was, in idleness, it was strange
How he cleared that sandal-wood off his range.
From the morning light till the light expired,

He was always working, he never tired ;
Till at length I began to think his will
Was too much settled on wealth, and still
When I looked at the lad's brown face, and eye
Clear open, my heart gave such thought the lie.
But one day—for he read my mind—he laid
His hand on my shoulder : "Don't be afraid,"
Said he, "that I'm seeking alone for pelf,
I work hard, friend ; but 'tis not for myself."
And he told me then, in his quiet tone,
Of a girl in Scotland, who was his own,—
His wife,—'twas for her : 'twas all he could say,
And his clear eye brimmed as he turned away.
After that he told me the simple tale :
They had married for love, and she was to sail
For Australia when he wrote home and told
The oft-watched-for story of finding gold.

In a year he wrote, and his news was good :
He had bought some cattle and sold his wood.
He said, "Darling, I've only a hut,—but come."
Friend, a husband's heart is a true wife's home ;
And he knew she'd come.   Then he turned his hand
To make neat the house, and prepare the land
For his crops and vines ; and he made that place
Put on such a smiling, home-like face,
That when she came, and he showed her round
His sandal wood and his crops in the ground,
And spoke of the future, they cried for joy,
The husband's arm clasping his wife and boy.

Well, friend, if a little of heaven's best bliss
Ever comes from the upper world to this,
It came into that manly bushman's life,
And circled him round with the arms of his wife.
God bless that bright memory !   Even to me,

A rough, lonely man, did she seem to be,
While living, an angel of God's pure love,
And now I could pray to her face above.
And David he loved her as only a man
With a heart as large as was his heart can.
I wondered how they could have lived apart,
For he was her idol, and she his heart.

Friend, there isn't much more of the tale to tell :
I was talking of angels awhile since.   Well,
Now I'll change to a devil,—ay, to a devil !
You needn't start : if a spirit of evil
Ever came to this world its hate to slake
On mankind, it came as a Dukite Snake.

Like ?   Like the pictures you've seen of Sin,
A long red snake,—as if what was within
Was fire that gleamed through his glistening skin,
And his eyes !—If you could go down to hell
And come back to your fellows here and tell
What the fire was like, you could find nothing,
Here below on the earth, or up in the sky,
To compare it to but a Dukite's eye !

Now, mark you, these Dukites don't go alone :
There's another near when you see but one ;
And beware you of killing that one you see
Without finding the other ; for you may be
More than twenty miles from the spot that night,
When camped, but you're tracked by the lone Dukite.
That will follow your trail like Death or Fate,
And kill you as sure as you killed its mate !

Well, poor Dave Sloane had his young wife here
Three months,—'twas just this time of the year.
He had teemed some sandal-wood to the basse,
And was homeward bound, when he saw in the grass

A long red snake : he had never been told
Of the Dukite's ways,—he jumped to the road,
And smashed its flat head with the bullock-goad !

He was proud of the red skin, so he tied
Its tail to the cart, and the snake's blood dyed
The bush on the path he followed that night.
He was early home, and the dead Dukite
Was flung at the door to be skinned next day.
At sunrise next morning he started away
To hunt up his cattle.   A three hours' ride
Brought him back : he gazed on his home with pride
And joy in his heart : he jumped from his horse
And entered—to look on his young wife's corse,
And his dead child clutching its mother's clothes
As in fright ; and there, as he gazed, arose
From her breast, where 'twas resting, the gleaming head
Of the terrible Dukite, as if it said,
" *I've had vengeance, my foe ; you took all I had.*"

And so had the snake—David Sloane was mad !
I rode to his hut just by chance that night,
And there on the threshold the clear moonlight
Showed the two snakes dead.   I pushed in the door
With an awful feeling of coming woe :
The dead were stretched on the moonlit floor,
The man held the hand of his wife,—his pride,
His poor life's treasure,—and crouched by her side.
O God ! I sank with the weight of the blow.
I touched and called him : he heeded me not,
So I dug her grave in a quiet spot,
And lifted them both,—her boy on her breast—
And laid them down in the shade to rest.
Then I tried to take my poor friend away,
But he cried so wofully, " Let me stay

Till she comes again ! " that I had no heart
To try to persuade him then to part
From all that was left to him here,—her grave ;
So I stayed by his side that night, and, save
One heart-cutting cry, he uttered no sound,—
O God ! that wail—like the wail of a hound !

'Tis six long years since I heard that cry,
But 'twill ring in my ears till the day I die.
Since that fearful night no one has heard
Poor David Sloane utter sound or word.
You have seen to-day how he always goes :
He's been given that suit of convict's clothes
By some prison officer.   On his back
You noticed a load like a pedlar's pack ?
Well, that's what he lives for : when reason went,
Still memory lived, for his days are spent
In searching for Dukites ; and year by year
That bundle of skins is growing.   'Tis clear
That the Lord out of evil some good still takes ;
For he's clearing this bush of the Dukite snakes.

John Boyle O'Reilly.

THE DOG GUARD.

AN AUSTRALIAN STORY.

THERE are lonesome places upon the earth
That have never re-echoed a sound of mirth,
Where the spirits abide that feast and quaff
On the shuddering soul of a murdered laugh,
And take grim delight in the fearful start,
As their unseen fingers clutch the heart,

And the blood flies out from the griping pain,
To carry the chill through every vein ;
And the staring eyes and the whitened faces
Are a joy to these ghosts of the lonesome places.

But of all the spots on this earthly sphere,
Where these dismal spirits are strong and near,
There is one more dreary than all the rest—
'Tis the barren island of Rottenest.
On Australia's western coast, you may—
On a seaman's chart of Fremantle Bay—
Find a tiny speck, some ten miles from shore :
If the chart be good, there is nothing more,—
For a shoal runs in on the landward side,
With five fathoms marked for the highest tide.
You have nought but my word for all the rest,
But that speck is the island of Rottenest.
'Tis a white sand-heap, about two miles long,
And say half as wide ; but the deeds of wrong
Between man and his brother that there took place
Are sufficient to sully a continent's face.
Ah, cruel tales ! were they told as a whole,
They would scare your polished humanity's soul ;
They would blanch the cheeks in your carpeted room,
With a terrible thought of the merited doom
For the crimes committed, still unredrest,
On that white sand-heap called Rottenest.

Of late years the island is not so bare
As it was when I saw it first ; for there
On the outer headland some buildings stand,
And a flag, red-crossed, say the patch of sand
Is a recognised part of the wide domain
That is blessed with the peace of Victoria's reign.
But behind the lighthouse the land's the same,
And it bears grim proof of the white man's shame ;

For the miniature vales that the island owns
Have a horrible harvest of human bones !

And how did they come there? that's the word ;
And I'll answer it now with the tale I heard
From the lips of a man who was there, and saw
The bad end of man's greed and of colony law.
Many years ago, when the white man first
Set his foot on the coast, and was hated and cursed
By the native, who had not yet learned to fear
The dark wrath of the stranger, but drove his spear
With a foeman's force and a bushman's yell
At the white invader, it then befell
That so many were killed, and cooked and eaten,
There was risk of the whites in the end being beaten ;
So a plan was proposed,—'twas deem'd safest and best
To imprison the natives in Rottenest.

And so every time there was white blood spilled,
There were black men captured ; and those not killed
In the rage of vengeance were sent away
To this black sand isle in Fremantle Bay ;
And it soon came round that a thousand men
Were together there, like wild beasts in a pen.
There was not a shrub or grass-blade in the sand,
Nor a piece of timber as large as your hand ;
But a government boat went out each day
To fling meat ashore—and then sailed away.

For a year or so was this course pursued,
Till 'twas noticed that fewer came down for food
When the boat appeared ; then a guard lay round
The island one night, and the white men found
That the savages swam at the lowest tide
To the shoal that lay on the landward side,—

'Twas a mile from the beach,—and then waded ashore ;
So the settlers met in grave council once more.

That a guard was needed was plain to all ;
But nobody answered the Governor's call
For a volunteer watch.   They were only a few,
And their wild young farms gave plenty to do ;
And the council of settlers was breaking up,
With a dread of the sorrow they'd have to sup
When the savage, unawed, and for vengeance wild,
Lay await in the wood for mother and child.
And with doleful countenance each to his neighbour
Told a dreary tale of the world of labour
He had, and said, "Let him watch who can,
I can't ; " when there stepped to the front a man
With a hard brown face and a burglar's brow,
Who had learned the secret he uttered now
When he served in the chain-gang in New South Wales.
And he said to them : " Friends, as all else fails,
These 'ere natives are safe as if locked and barred,
If you'll line that shoal with a mastiff guard ! "

And the settlers looked at each other awhile,
Till the wonder toned to a well-pleased smile
When the brown ex-burglar said he knew,
And would show the whole of 'em what to do.
Some three weeks after the guard was set ;
And a native who swam to the shoal was met
By two half-starved dogs, when a mile from shore,—
And, somehow, that native was never seen more.
All the settlers were pleased with the capital plan,
And they voted their thanks to the hard-faced man.
For a year each day did the government boat
Take the meat to the isle and its guard afloat.
In a line, on the face of the shoal, the dogs
Had a dry house each, on some anchored logs ;

And the neck-chain from each stretched just half-way
To the next dog's house ; right across the Bay
Ran a line that was hideous with sounds
From the hungry throats of two hundred hounds.

So one year passed, and the brutes on the logs
Had grown more like devils than common dogs.
There was such a hell-chorus by day and night
That the settlers ashore were chilled with fright
When they thought—if that legion should break away,
And come in with the tide some fatal day !

But they 'scaped that chance ; for a man came in
From the Bush, one day, with a 'possum skin
To the throat filled up with large pearls he'd found
To the north, on the shore of the Shark's Bay Sound.
And the settlement blazed with a wild commotion
At sight of the gems from the wealthy ocean.

Then the settlers all began to pack
Their tools and tents, and to ask the track
That the bushman followed to strike the spot,—
While the dogs and natives were all forgot.
In two days, from that camp on the River Swan,
To the Shark's Bay Sound had the settlers gone ;
And no merciful feeling did one retard
For the helpless men and their terrible guard.

It were vain to try, in my quiet room,
To write down the truth of the awful doom
That befell those savages prisoned there,
When the pangs of hunger and wild despair
Had nigh made them mad as the fiends outside :
'Tis enough that one night, through the low ebb-tide,
Swam nine hundred savages, armed with stones
And with weapons made from their dead friends' bones.

Without ripple or sound, when the moon was gone,
Through the inky water they glided on ;
Swimming deep and scarce daring to draw a breath,
While the guards, if they saw, were as dumb as death.

'Twas a terrible picture !   O.God ! that the night
Were so black as to cover the horrid sight
From the eyes of the Angel that notes man's ways
In the book that will ope on the Day of Days ! [pain !
There were screams when they met,—shrill screams of
For each animal swam at the length of his chain,
And with parching throat and in furious mood
Lay awaiting, not men, but his coming food.
There were short, sharp cries, and a line of fleck
As the long fangs sank in the swimmer's neck ;
There were gurgling growls mixed with human groans,
For the savages drave the sharpened bones
Through their enemies' ribs, and the bodies sank,
Each dog holding fast with a bone through his flank.

Then those of the natives who 'scaped swam back ;
But too late ! for scores of the savage pack,
Driven mad by the yells and the sounds of fight,
Had broke loose and followed.   On that dread night
Let the curtain fall : when the red sun rose
From the placid ocean, the joys and woes
Of a thousand men he had last eve seen
Were as things or thoughts that had never been.

When the settlers returned,—in a month or two,—
They bethought of the dogs and the prisoned crew,
And a boat went out on a tardy quest
Of whatever was living on Rottenest.
They searched all the isle, and sailed back again
With some specimen bones of the dogs and men.

                                    John Boyle O'Reilly.

THE AMBER WHALE.

A HARPOONER'S STORY.

WE were down in the Indian Ocean, after sperm, and
  three years out ;
The last six months in the tropics, and looking in vain
  for a spout,—
Five men up on the royal yards, weary of straining their
  sight ;
And every day like its brother,—just morning and noon
  and night—
Nothing to break the sameness : water and wind and
  sun
Motionless, gentle, and blazing,—never a change in one.
Every day like its brother : when the noonday eight-
  bells came,
'Twas like yesterday; and we seemed to know that
  to-morrow would be the same.
The foremast hands had a lazy time : there was never a
  thing to do ;
The ship was painted, tarred down, and scraped ; and
  the mates had nothing new.
We'd worked at sinnet and ratline till there wasn't a
  yarn to use,
And all we could do was watch and pray for a sperm
  whale's spout—or news.
It was whaler's luck of the vilest sort ; and, though
  many a volunteer
Spent his watch below on the look-out, never a whale
  came near,—
At least of the kind we wanted : there were lots of whales
  of a sort,—
Killers and finbacks, and such like, as if they enjoyed
  the sport

Of seeing a whale-ship idle; but we never lowered a
  boat
For less than a blackfish,—there's no oil in a killer's or
  finback's coat.
There was rich reward for the look-out men,—tobacco for
  even a sail,
And a barrel of oil for the lucky dog who'd be first to
  " raise " a whale.
The crew was a mixture from every land, and many a
  tongue they spoke ;
And when they sat in the fo'castle, enjoying an evening
  smoke,
There were tales told, youngster, would make you stare,
  —stories of countless shoals
Of devil-fish in the Pacific and right-whales away at the
  Poles.
There was one of these fo'castle yarns that we always
  loved to hear,—
Kanaka and Maori and Yankee ; all lent an eager ear
To that strange old tale that was always new,—the
  wonderful treasure-tale
Of an old Down-Eastern harpooneer who had struck an
  Amber Whale !
Ay, that was a tale worth hearing, lad : if 'twas true we
  couldn't say,
Or if 'twas a yarn old Mat had spun to while the time
  away.

" It's just fifteen years ago," said Mat, " since I shipped
  as harpooneer
On board a bark in New Bedford, and came cruising
  somewhere near
To this whaling-ground we're cruising now ; but whales
  were plenty then,
And not like now, when we scarce get oil to pay for the
  ship and men.

There were none of these oil wells running then,—at
least, what shore folk term
An oil well in Pennsylvania,—but sulphur-bottom and
sperm
Were plenty as frogs in a mud-hole, and all of 'em big
whales too,
One hundred barrels for sperm-whale ; and for sulphur-
bottom two.
You couldn't pick out a small one : the littlest calf or
cow
Had a sight more oil than the big bull whales we think
so much of now.
We were more to the east, off Java Straits, a little below
the mouth,—
A hundred and five to the east'ard and nine degrees to
the south ;
And that was as good a whaling-ground for middling-
sized, handy whales
As any in all the ocean ; and 'twas always white with
sails
From Scotland and Hull and New England,—for the
whales were thick as frogs,
And 'twas little trouble to kill 'em then, for they lay as
quiet as logs.
And every night we'd go visiting the other whale ships
'round,
Or p'r'aps we'd strike on a Dutchman, calmed off the
Straits, and bound
To Singapore or Batavia, with plenty of schnapps to
sell
For a few whale's teeth or a gallon of oil, and the latest
news to tell.
And in every ship of that whaling fleet was one wonderful
story told,—
How an Amber Whale had been seen that year that was
worth a mint of gold.

And one man—mate of a Scotchman—said he'd seen,
   away to the west,
A big school of sperm, and one whale's spout was twice
   as high as the rest ;
And we knew that that was the Amber Whale, for we'd
   often heard before
That his spout was twice as thick as the rest, and a
   hundred feet high or more.
And often, when the look-out cried, 'He blows!' the
   very hail
Thrilled every heart with greed of gold,—for we thought
   of the Amber Whale.

"But never a sight of his spout we saw till the season
   there went round,
And the ships ran down to the south'ard to another
   whaling-ground.
We stayed to the last off Java, and then we ran to the
   west,
To get our recruits at Mauritius, and give the crew a rest.
Five days we ran in the trade winds ; and the boys were
   beginning to talk
Of their time ashore, and whether they'd have a donkey-
   ride or a walk,
And whether they'd spend their money in wine, bananas,
   or pearls,
Or drive to the sugar plantations to dance with the Creole
   girls.
But they soon got something to talk about.   Five days
   we ran west-sou'-west,
But the sixth day's log-book entry was a change from all
   the rest ;
For that was the day the mast-head men made every face
   turn pale,
With the cry that we all had dreamt about,—'*He blows!
   the Amber Whale!*'

" And every man was motionless, and every speaker's
    lip
Just stopped as it was, with the word half-said : there
    wasn't a sound in the ship
Till the Captain hailed the masthead, ' Whereaway is the
    whale you see? '
And the cry came down again, ' He blows I about four
    points on our lee,
And three miles off, sir,—there he blows I he's going to
    leaward fast ! '
And then we sprang to the rigging, and saw the great
    whale at last I

" Ah I shipmates, that was a sight to see : the water was
    smooth as a lake,
And there was the monster rolling, with a school of
    whales in his wake.
They looked like pilot-fish round a shark, as if they were
    keeping guard ;
And, shipmates, the spout of that Amber Whale was
    high as a sky-sail yard.
There was never a ship's crew worked so quick as our
    whalemen worked that day,—
When the captain shouted, ' Swing the boats, and be
    ready to lower away ! '
Then, ' A pull on the weather-braces, men ! let her head
    fall off three points ! '
And off she swung, with a quarter-breeze straining the
    old ship's joints.
The men came down from the mastheads ; and the boats'
    crews stood on the rail,
Stowing the lines and irons, and fixing paddles and sail.
And when all was ready we leant on the boats and
    looked at the Amber's spout,
That went up like a monster fountain, with a sort of a
    rambling shout,

Like a thousand railroad engines puffing away their smoke.
He was just like a frigate's hull capsized, and the water
    swaying broke
Against the sides of the great stiff whale : he was steering
    south-by-west,—
For the Cape, no doubt, for a whale can shape a course
    as well as the best.
We soon got close as was right to go ; for the school
    might hear a hail,
Or see the bark, and that was the last of our Bank-of-
    England Whale.
' Let her luff,' said the Old Man, gently. ' Now, lower
    away, my boys,
And pull for a mile, then paddle,—and mind that you
    make no noise.'

"A minute more, and the boats were down ; and out
    from the hull of the bark
They shot with a nervous sweep of the oars, like dolphins
    away from a shark.
Each officer stood in the stern, and watched, as he held
    the steering oar,
And the crews bent down to their pulling as they never
    pulled before.

"Our Mate was as thorough a whaleman as I ever met
    afloat ;
And I was his harpooner that day, and sat in the bow of
    the boat.
His eyes were set on the whales ahead, and he spoke in
    a low, deep tone,
And told the men to be steady and cool, and the whale
    was all our own.
And steady and cool they proved to be : you could read
    it on every face,

And in every straining muscle, that they meant to win
  that race.
' Bend to it, boys, for a few strokes more,—bend to it
  steady and long !
Now in with your oars, and paddles out,—all together,
  and strong !'
Then we turned and sat on the gunwale, with our faces
  to the bow ;
And the whales were right ahead,—no more than four
  ships' lengths off now.
There were five of 'em, hundred barrellers, like guards
  round the Amber Whale,
And to strike him we'd have to risk being stove by
  crossing a sweeping tail ;
But the prize and the risk were equal.   ' Mat,' now
  whispers the Mate,
' Are your irons ready ?'   ' Ay, ay, sir.'   ' Stand up then,
  steady, and wait
Till I give the word, then let 'em fly, and hit him below
  the fin
As he rolls to wind'ard.   Start her, boys ! now's the
  time to slide her in !
Hurrah ! that fluke just missed us.   Mind, as soon as
  the iron's fast,
Be ready to back your paddles,—now in for it, boys, at
  last.
Heave !   Again !'

"And two irons flew : the first one sank in the
  point,
'Tween the head and the hump,—in the muscle ; but the
  second had its point
Turned off by striking the amber case, coming out again
  like a bow,
And the monster carcass quivered, and rolled with pain
  from the first deep blow.

Then he lashed the sea with his terrible flukes, and
  showed us many a sign
That his rage was roused. ' Lay off,' roared the Mate,
  ' and all keep clear of the line ! '
And that was a timely warning, for the whale made an
  awful breach
Right out of the sea ; and 'twas well for us that the boat
  was beyond the reach
Of his sweeping flukes, as he milled around, and made
  for the Captain's boat,
That was right astern. And, shipmates, then my heart
  swelled up in my throat
At the sight I saw : the Amber Whale was lashing the
  sea with rage,
And two of his hundred-barrel guards were ready now
  to engage
In a bloody fight, and with open jaws they came to
  their master's aid.
Then we knew that the Captain's boat was doomed ;
  but the crew were no whit afraid.—
They were brave New England whalemen,—and we saw
  the harpooner
Stand up to send his irons, as soon as the whale came near.
Then we heard the Captain's order, ' Heave ! ' and saw
  the harpoon fly,
As the whales closed in with their open jaws : a shock,
  and a stifled cry,
Was all that we heard ; then we looked to see if the
  crew were still afloat,—
But nothing was there save a dull red patch, and the
  boards of the shattered boat !

" But there was no time for mourning words : the other
  two boats came in,
And one got fast on the quarter, and one aft the starboard
  fin

Of the Amber Whale.   For a minute he paused, as if
   he were in doubt
As to whether 'twas best to run or fight.   ' Lay on ! '
   the Mate roared out,
' And I'll give him a lance ! '   The boat shot in ; and
   the Mate, when he saw his chance
Of sending it home to the vitals, four times he buried
   his lance.
A minute more, and a cheer went up, when we saw that
   his aim was good ;
For the lance had struck in a life-spot, and the whale
   was spouting blood !
But now came the time of danger, for the school of
   whales around
Had aired their flukes, and the cry was raised, ' Look
   out ! they're going to sound ! '
And down they went with a sudden plunge, the Amber
   Whale the last,
While the lines ran smoking out of the tubs, he went to
   the deep so fast.
Before you could count your fingers, a hundred fathoms
   were out ;
And then he stopped, for a wounded whale must come to
   the top to spout.
We hauled slack line as we felt him rise ; and when he
   came up alone,
And spouted thick blood, we cheered again, for we knew
   he was all our own.
He was frightened now, and his fight was gone,—right
   round and round he spun,
As if he was trying to sight the boats, or find the best
   side to run.
But that was the minute for us to work : the boats
   hauled in their slack,
And bent on the drag-tubs over the stern, to tire and
   hold him back.

500

The bark was five miles to wind'ard, and the Mate gave
    a troubled glance
At the sinking sun, and muttered, ' Boys, we must give
    him another lance,
Or he'll run till night ; and, if he should head to the
    wind'ard in the dark,
We'll be forced to cut loose and leave him, or else lose
    run of the bark.'
So we hauled in close, two boats at once, but only
    frightened the whale ;
And like a hound that was badly whipped, he turned
    and showed his tail,
With his head right dead to wind'ard ; then as straight
    and swift he sped
As a hungry shark for a swimming prey ; and bending
    over his head,
Like a mighty plume, went his bloody spout.   Ah ! ship-
    mates, that was a sight
Worth a life at sea to witness.   In his wake the sea was
    white
As you've seen it after a steamer's screw, churning up
    like foaming yeast ;
And the boats went hissing along at the rate of twenty
    knots at least.
With the water flush with the gunwale, and the oars
    were all apeak,
While the crews sat silent and quiet, watching the long
    white streak
That was traced by the line of our passage.   We hailed
    the bark as we passed,
And told them to keep a sharp look-out from the head of
    every mast ;
' And if we're not back by sundown,' cried the Mate,
    ' you keep a light
At the royal cross-trees.   If he dies, we may stick to the
    whale all night.'

" And past we swept with our oars apeak, and waved our
hands to the hail
Of the wondering men on the taffrail, who were watching
our Amber Whale
As he surged ahead, just as if he thought he could tire
his enemies out ;
I was almost sorrowful, shipmates, to see after each red
spout
That the great whale's strength was failing : the sweep of
his flukes grew slow,
Till at sundown he made about four knots, and his spout
was weak and low.
Then said the Mate to his boat's crew : ' Boys, the vessel
is out of sight
To the leeward : now, shall we cut the line, or stick to
the whale all night ?'
' We'll stick to the whale ! cried every man. ' Let the
other boats go back
To the vessel and beat to wind'ard, as well as they can in
our track.'
It was done as they said : the lines were cut, and the
crews cried out, ' God speed ! '
As we swept along in the darkness, in the wake of our
monster steed,
That went plunging on, with the dogged hope that he'd
tire his enemies still,—
But even the strength of an Amber Whale must break
before human will.
By little and little his power had failed as he spouted his
blood away,
Till at midnight the rising moon looked down on the
great fish as he lay
Just moving his flukes ; but at length he stopped, and
raising his square black head
As high as the topmast cross-trees, swung round and fell
over—dead !

And then rose a shout of triumph,—a shout that was more
    like a curse
Than an honest cheer ; but, shipmates, the thought in
    our hearts was worse,
And 'twas punished with bitter suffering.   We claimed
    the whale as our own,
And said that the crew should have no share of the wealth
    that was ours alone.
We said to each other : We want their help till we get
    the whale aboard,
So we'll let them think that they'll have a share till we
    get the Amber stored,
And then we'll pay them their wages, and send them
    ashore—*or afloat,*
If they show their temper.   Oh ! shipmates, no wonder
    'twas that boat
And its selfish crew were cursed that night.   Next day
    we saw no sail,
But the wind and sea were rising.   Still we held to the
    drifting whale,—
And a dead whale drifts to windward,—going further
    away from the ship,
Without water, or bread, or courage to pray with heart
    or lip
That had planned or spoken the treachery.   The wind
    blew into a gale,
And it screamed like mocking laughter round our boat
    and the Amber Whale.

"Then night fell dark on the starving crew, and a
    hurricane blew next day ;
Then we cut the line, and we cursed the prize as it drifted
    fast away,
As if some power under the waves were towing it out of
    sight ;

And there we were, without help or hope, dreading the
  coming night.
Three days that hurricane lasted. When it passed, two
  men were dead ;
And the strongest one of the living had not strength to
  raise his head,
When his dreaming swoon was broken by the sound of a
  cheery hail,
And he saw a shadow fall on the boat,—it fell from the
  old bark's sail !
And when he heard their kindly words, you'd think he
  might have smiled
With joy at his deliverance ; but he cried like a little
  child,
And hid his face in his poor weak hands,—for he thought
  of the selfish plan,—
And he prayed to God to forgive them all. And, ship-
  mates, I am the man !—
The only one of the sinful crew that ever beheld his
  home ;
For before the cruise was over, all the rest were under
  the foam.
It's just fifteen years gone, shipmates," said old Mat,
  ending his tale ;
" And I often pray that I'll never see another Amber
  Whale."

John Boyle O'Reilly.

A SAVAGE.

DIXON, a Choctaw, twenty years of age,
  Had killed a miner in a Leadville brawl ;
Tried and condemned, the rough-beards curb their rage,
  And watch him stride in freedom from the hall.

"*Return on Friday, to be shot to death !*"
So ran the sentence—it was Monday night,
The dead man's comrades drew a well-pleased breath;
    Then all night long the gambling dens were bright.

The days sped slowly; but the Friday came,
    And flocked the miners to the shooting-ground;
They chose six riflemen of deadly aim,
    And with low voices sat and lounged around.

"He will not come." "He's not a fool." "The men
    Who set the savage free must face the blame."
A Choctaw brave smiled bitterly, and then
    Smiled proudly, with raised head, as Dixon came,

Silent and stern—a woman at his heels;
    He motions to the brave, who stays her tread.
Next minute—flame the guns: the woman reels
    And drops without a moan—Dixon is dead.

                                    John Boyle O'Reilly.

THE RANCHMAN'S BRIDAL.

I. CAST by the life of care, love;
        Course o'er the plains with me;
    Hard is a plainsman's fare, love,
        Bold is the life and free;
    Thou art a plainsman's mate, love,
        Wedded in heart and hand;
    Horses are at the gate love,
        Priests at the altar stand.

        Chorus.—So silver spurs are ringing
                    A wedding chime to-day,
                    And all the birds are singing
                    One blithesome roundelay.

II. Queen of the boundless range, love !
    Down by the shady branch,
 Peace that shall never change, love,
    Nests in the lonely ranche ;
 Roses are in the glade, love,
    And ripples ride the stream ;
 But out beyond the shade, love,
    The silver waters gleam.

  Chorus.—So silver spurs, etc.

III. Brighter the hearth and wide, love,
     When children bid you say
 How we rode side by side, love,
    Upon our bridal day,
 And shared our hopes and fears, love,
    And shared the sun and rain,
 As we rode through the years, love,
    Across life's joyous plain !

  Chorus.—So silver spurs, etc.

      H. R. A. Pocock.

AFAR IN THE DESERT.

AFAR in the Desert I love to ride,
With the silent Bush-boy alone by my side :
When the sorrows of life the soul o'ercast,
And, sick of the Present, I cling to the Past ;
When the eye is suffused with regretful tears,
From the fond recollections of former years ;
And shadows of things that have long since fled
Flit over the brain, like ghosts of the dead :
Bright visions of glory—that vanished too soon ;
Day dreams—that departed ere manhood's noon ;

Attachments—by fate or by falsehood reft ;
Companions of early days—lost or left ;
And my Native Land—whose magical name
Thrills to the heart like electric flame ;
The home of my childhood, the haunts of my prime;
All the passions and scenes of that rapturous time
When the feelings were young and the world was
    new,
Like the fresh bowers of Eden unfolding to view ;
All—all now forsaken—forgotten—foregone !
And I—a lone exile remembered of none—
My high aims abandoned,—my good acts undone,—
Aweary of all that is under the sun,—
Wih that sadness of heart which no stranger may
    scan,
I fly to the Desert, afar from man.

Afar in the Desert I love to ride,
With the silent Bush-boy alone by my side :
When the wild turmoil of this wearisome life,
With its scenes of oppression, corruption, and strife—
The proud man's frown, and the base man's fear,—
The scorner's laugh, and the sufferer's tear,—
And malice, and meanness, and falsehood, and folly,
Dispose me to musing and dark melancholy ;
When my bosom is full, and my thoughts are high,
And my soul is sick with the bondman's sigh—
Oh ! then there is freedom, and joy, and pride,
Afar in the Desert alone to ride !
There is rapture to vault on the champing steed,
And to bound away with the eagle's speed,
With the death-fraught firelock in my hand—
The only law in the Desert Land !

Afar in the Desert I love to ride,
With the silent Bush-boy alone by my side :

Away—away from the dwellings of men,
By the wild deer's haunt, by the buffalo's glen ;
By valleys remote where the oribi plays,
Where the gnu, the gazelle, and the hartébeest graze,
Where the kùdù and eland unhunted recline
By the skirts of grey forests o'erhung with wild vine ;
Where the elephant browses at peace in his wood,
And the river-horse gambols unscared in the flood,
And the mighty rhinoceros wallows at will
In the fen where the wild-ass is drinking his fill.

Afar in the Desert I love to ride,
With the silent Bush-boy alone by my side :
O'er the brown Karroo, where the bleating cry
Of the springbok's fawn sounds plaintively ;
And the timorous quagga's shrill whistling neigh
Is heard by the fountain at twilight grey ;
Where the zebra wantonly tosses his mane,
With wild hoof scouring the desolate plain ;
And the fleet-footed ostrich over the waste
Speeds like a horseman who travels in haste,
Hieing away to the home of her rest,
Where she and her mate have scooped their nest,
Far hid from the pitiless plunderer's view
In the pathless depths of the parched Karroo.

Afar in the Desert I love to ride,
With the silent Bush-boy alone by my side :
Away—away—in the Wilderness vast,
Where the White Man's foot hath never passed,
And the quivered Coránna or Bechuán
Hath rarely crossed with his roving clan :
A region of emptiness, howling and drear,
Which Man hath abandoned from famine and fear ;
Which the snake and the lizard inhabit alone,
With the twilight bat from the yawning stone ;

"*QUELLING OF THE MOOSE.*"

Where grass, nor herb, nor shrub takes root,
Save poisonous thorns that pierce the foot ;
And the bitter-melon, for food and drink,
Is the pilgrim's fare by the salt lake's brink :
A region of drought, where no river glides,
Nor rippling brook with osiered sides ;
Where sedgy pool, nor bubbling fount,
Nor tree, nor cloud, nor misty mount,
Appears, to refresh the aching eye :
But the barren earth, and the burning sky,
And the blank horizon, round and round
Spread—void of living sight and sound.
And here, while the night-winds round me sigh,
And the stars burn bright in the midnight sky,
As I sit apart by the desert stone,
Like Elijah at Horeb's cave alone,
" A still small voice " comes through the wild
(Like a Father consoling his fretful child)
Which banishes bitterness, wrath, and fear,—
Saying—Man is distant, but God is near !

Thomas Pringle.

"THE QUELLING OF THE MOOSE."

[A MELICITE LEGEND.]

WHEN tent was pitched, and supper done,
And forgotten were paddle, and rod, and gun,
And the low, bright planets, one by one,

Lit in the pine-tops their lamps of gold,
To us by the fire, in our blankets rolled,
This was the story Sacòbi told :—

" In those days came the Moose from the east,
A monster out of the white north-east,
And as leaves before him were man and beast.

" The dark rock-hills of Saguenay
Are strong,—they were but straws in his way.
He leapt the St. Lawrence as in play.

" His breath was a storm and a flame ; his feet
In the mountains thundered, fierce and fleet,
Till men's hearts were as milk, and ceased to beat.

" But in those days dwelt Clote Scarp with men.
It is long to wait till he comes again,—
But a friend was near, and could hear us, then !

" In his wigwam, built by the Dolastook,
Where the ash-trees over the water look,
A voice of trouble the stillness shook.

" He rose, and took his bow from the wall,
And listened ; he heard his people's call
Pierce up from the villages one and all.

" From village to village he passed with cheer,
And the people followed ; but when drew near
The stride of the Moose, they fled in fear.

" Like smoke in a wind they fled at the last.
But he in a pass of the hills stood fast,
And down at his feet his bow he cast.

" That terrible forehead, maned with flame,
He smote with his open hand,—and tame
As a dog the raging beast became.

" He smote with his open hand ; and lo !
As shrinks in the rains of spring the snow,
So shrank the monster beneath that blow,

"Till scarce the bulk of a bull he stood,
And Clote Scarp led him down to the wood,
And gave him the tender shoots for food."

He ceased.   And a voice said, " Understand
How huge a peril will shrink like sand,
When stayed by a prompt and steady hand."

Charles G. D. Roberts.

HOW THE MOKAWKS SET OUT FOR MEDOCTEC.

[When the invading Mohawks captured the outlying Melicite village of Madawaska, they spared two squaws to guide them down to the main Melicite town of Medoctec, below Grand Falls.   The squaws steered themselves and their captors over the Falls.]

I.

Grows the great deed, though none
Shout to behold it done !
To the brave deed done by night
Heaven testifies in the light !

Stealthy and swift as a dream,
Crowding the breast of the stream,
In their paint and plumes of war
And their war-canoes four score,

They are threading the Oolastook
Where his cradling hills o'erlook.
The branchy thickets hide them ;
The unstartled waters guide them.

II.

Comes night to the quiet hills
Where the Madawaska spills,—
To his slumbering huts no warning,
Nor mirth of another morning !

No more shall the children wake
As the dawns through the hut-door break ;
But the dogs, a trembling pack,
With wistful eyes steal back.

And, to pilot the noiseless foe
Through the perilous passes, go
Two women who could not die —
Whom the knife in the dark passed by.

III.

Where the shoaling waters froth,
Churned thick like devils' broth,—
Where the rocky shark-jaw waits,
Never a bark that grates.

And the tearless captives' skill
Contents them.   Onward still !
And the low-voiced captives' tell
The tidings that cheer them well:

How a clear stream leads them down
Well-nigh to Medoctec town,
Ere to the great Falls' thunder
The long wall yawns asunder.

IV.

The clear stream glimmers before them ;
The faint night falters o'er them ;
Lashed lightly bark to bark,
They glide the windless dark.

Late grows the night.   No fear
While the skilful captives steer !
Sleeps the tired warrior, sleeps
The chief; and the river creeps.

V.

In the town of the Melicite
The unjarred peace is sweet,
Green grows the corn and great,
And the hunt is fortunate.

This many a heedless year
The Mohawks come not near.
The lodge-gate stands unbarred ;
Scarce even a dog keeps guard.

No mother shrieks from a dream
Of blood on the threshold stream,--
But the thought of those mute guides
Is where the sleeper bides !

VI.

Gets forth those caverned walls
No roar from the giant Falls,
Whose mountainous foam treads under
The abyss of awful thunder.

But—the river's sudden speed !
How the ghost-grey shores recede !
And the tearless pilots hear
A muttering voice creep near.

A tremor ! The blanched leap.
The warriors start from sleep.
Faints in the sudden blare
The cry of their swift despair.

And the captives' death-chant shrills.
But afar, remote from ills,
Quiet under the quiet skies
The Melicite village lies.

Charles G. D. Roberts.

THE SNOWS.

[A RAPID ON THE UPPER OTTAWA.]

OVER the snows
Buoyantly goes
The lumberers' bark canoe ;
Lightly they sweep,
Wilder each leap,
Rending the white-caps through.
Away ! away !
With the speed of a startled deer,
While the steersman true,
And his laughing crew,
Sing of their wild career :

" Mariners glide
Far o'er the tide,
In ships that are staunch and strong;
Safely as they
Speed we away,
Waking the woods with song."
Away ! away !
With the speed of a startled deer,
While the laughing crew
Of the swift canoe
Sing of the raftsmen's cheer :

" Downward we dash,
Through lightning-flash,
Lightning, and sleet, and storm,
Skimming the wave
With hearts so brave,
While the life-blood circles warm.
Away ! away !
Like the stag in a race for life,
Though the wave rose higher,
Through a spray of fire,
And the sky were wild with strife.

Over the snows
Buoyantly goes
The lumberers' bark canoe ;
Lightly they sweep,
Wilder each leap,
Tearing the white-caps through.
Away ! away !
With the speed of a startled deer ;
There's a fearless crew .
In each light canoe,
To sing of the raftsmen's cheer.

Charles Sangster.

THE STOCK-DRIVER'S RIDE.

O'ER the range, and down the gully, across the river bed,
We are riding on the tracks of the cattle that have fled :
The mopokes all are laughing, and the cockatoos are
    screaming,
And bright amidst the stringy-barks the parrakeets are
gleaming :

The wattle-blooms are fragrant, and the great magnolias
    fair
Make a heavy, sleepy sweetness in the hazy morning air ;
But the rattle and the crashing of our horses' hoofs ring
    out,
And the cheery shout we answer with our long repeated
    shout—

Coo-ee-coo-ee-eee ! Coo-ee-coo-eee-Coo-ee-Coo-ee !
"Damnation Dick" he hears us, and he shrills back
    Whoo-ee-ee !
"Damnation Dick," the prince of native trackers thus we
    call,
From the way he swigs his liquor, and the oaths that he
can squall !

Thro' more ranges, thro' more gullies, down sun-scorch'd
    granite ways
We go crashing, slipping, thundering in our joyous
    morning race—
And the drowsy 'possums shriek, and o'er each dried-up
    creek
The wallabies run scuttling, as if playing hide-and-seek :

And like iron striking iron do our horses' hoofs loud
ring
As down the barren granite slopes we leap and slide and
spring;
Then one range further only and we each a moment
rein
Our steaming steeds, as wide before us stretches out the
grassy plain !

And "Damnation Dick" comes running like a human
kangaroo,
And he cries, "The herd have bolted to the creek of
Waharoo!"
So we swing across the desert, and for miles and miles we
go
Till men and horses pant athirst i' the fierce sun's fiery
glow.

And at last across the plains where the kangaroos fly
leaping,
And the startled emus in their flight go circularly
sweeping,
We see the trees that hide the spring of Waharoo, and
there
The cattle all are standing still—the bulls with a fierce
stare !

Then off to right goes Harry on his sorrel "Pretty
Jane,"
And to the left on "Thunderbolt" Tom scours across
the plain,
And Jim and I, well-mounted, and on foot "Damnation
Dick,"
Go straight for Waharoo, and our stockwhips fling and
flick !

THE ISLE OF LOVE.   163

Ho ! there goes old " Black-beetle," the patriarch of the
herd !
His doughty courage vanish'd when Tom's long leash
cracked and whirred ;
And after him the whole lot flee, and homeward headlong
dash—
What bellowing flight and thunder of hoofs as thro' the
scrub we crash !

Back through the gum-tree gullies, and over the river-
bed,
And past the sassafras ranges whereover at dawn we
sped ;
With thunderous noise and shouting the drivers and
driven flee—
And this was the race that was raced by Tom, Jim,
Harry, and me !

William Sharp.

GIPPSLAND, *January* 1877.

THE ISLE OF LOVE.

[FROM "THE HUMAN INHERITANCE."]

I.

A VAST deep dome wherein the shining fires
Of space hung panting, as though keen desires
Burn'd in them to spring forth from the blind force
That held them as in leash ; a comet's course
Blazed in the east, and constellations flamed
As through the night they strode ; the famed
Canopus, whom on Syrian wastes afar
Men once had worshipp'd, and the fiery star

Aldebaran, and, sword-girt, great Orion,
Whose light feared not the moon's—all these outshone
With splendour from dark heaven, and many more
Which mariners know well when drifting o'er
The far south seas : the Southern Cross agleam
With fire hung high, and, as in some fierce dream
A tigress pants, the pulsing star men know
As Sirius, in ever-changing glow,
Blood-red and purple, green, and blue, and white,
Flamed on the swarthy bosom of the night.

II.

As though the power that made the Nautilus
A living glory on the perilous
Wild seas to roam, had from the utmost deep
Call'd a vast, flawless peal from out its sleep,
And carved it crescentwise, exceeding fair,—
So seemed the crescent moon, that thro' the air
With motionless motion glided from the west,
And sailing onward ever seem'd at rest.

III.

Below, the wide waste of the ocean lay.
League upon league of moonled waters, spray
And foam and salt-sea send ; a world of sea
By strong winds buffeted.   And furtively
At times a shadow loomed above the waves
Only to fade, as men say out of graves
Troop spirits who flee back at mortal gaze ;
This shadow was a ship, which many days
Ago had pass'd the doleful straits where sleep
The storms that rage and ravin on the deep.
She seem'd a bird, black, with tremendous wings
Poised high above her, a condor bird that brings

Death in her sweep. Slowly the shadow grew
Distinct, and the stars seem'd more faint or few,
And the waves waxed wan and leaden, and afar
I' the east the night seem'd troubled : ev'ry spar
Stood forth in outline, and above the topmost sail
The delicate glory of the moon grew pale.

IV.

The night rose from the east, and with slow sweep
Her shadowy robes about her o'er the deep
Far westward floated ; the dusk, her sister fair,
With soft remembering eyes and twilight hair,
From out the brooding depths of heaven stole,
And linger'd with her faint sweet aureole
Of trembling light, as though she could not leave
The shadowy ways she haunted, where waves heave
As sighing in sleep, and as adream the wind
Breathes hushfully. But, lo ! the east behind
Quivers, and afar the horizon thrills
One moment, and a sea-bird wails and shrills,
Then sinks to rest again. And like a dream
That fades as we awake, or like the gleam
Upon a child's face ere it falls to sleep
The tender twilight faded o'er the deep.

V.

Again the whole east trembled, and a hush
Fill'd sky and sea ; and then a rosy flush
Stole upward, as sweet and delicately fair
As pink wild roses in the April air.
And suddenly some shafts of gold were hurled
Right up into the sky, and o'er the world
A molten flood seem'd imminent, till swift
The rose-veil parted in a mighty rift,

And the great sun sprang forth, and o'er the sea
Rose up resplendent, shining gloriously.

VI.

White shone the wind-fill'd sails of the tall ship
Escaping from the waves, fain to outstrip
This giant of the deep : a league behind
The white track she had made danced in the wind
Foaming and surging, while white clouds of spray
Swept from the bows that cleft their wind-urged way.

VII.

And suddenly a shout came from the crew,
For one had spied emerging from the blue
What seem'd a delicate pale purple band
Of morning cloud ; no larger than a hand
It lay asleep upon th' horizon line,
And like some lovely amethyst did shine.
But this was land, and eager eyes were bent
To take the wonder in.   Even then a scent
Of something sweeter than the salt sea-breeze
Seem'd in the air, odours of spicy trees
And sweet green grass, and fruits, and flow'rs the eye
Sees only 'neath the hot Pacific sky;
And every heart was glad, for each felt free
For one day from the ever-present sea.

VIII.

But after noon had passed with scorching rays,
The wind grew slack, and then a gauzy haze
Crept from the quivering north, and to and fro
Wandered the windless waves, as white sheep go
Straggling about the meadow-lands when far
The shepherd strays ; and from the distant bar,

White in both calm and tempest, that enwound
What now was seen an island, came the sound
Of breaking billows in a muffled roar,
As in a shell one hears a wave-washed shore.
And soon the sea itself grew still and mild,
And seem'd to sleep, just as a little child
After its boisterous play and fretful rest
Lays down its head upon its mother's breast
And, smiling, becomes one of God's pure things
Once more : and as with folded wings
An angel sleeps upon the buoyant air,
So wholly slept the wind ; while with her hair
A misty veil about her, Silence rose
And cast o'er sea and sky her hush'd repose.

IX.

As a dream slowly onward drifts to sleep,
So stealthily the windless ship did creep
Closer and closer to the foaming bar ;
Noon burned above, like furnace vast afar
Flaming unseen ; and, with a dazzling glare,
The sleeping ocean heaved her bosom bare
As some great woman of the giant days,
Supine 'mid mountain-grasses in the rays
Of an intolerable sun, might breathe
With panting breasts ; far in cool depths beneath
'Mid swaying loveliness of ocean weed
Bright fish swarm to and fro, and with fell speed,
The pale shark gleamed and vanish'd as when Death
Is seen a moment 'mid life's failing breath.

X.

At last a boat put off from the ship's side,
Urged by swift oars,—a speck upon the wide

And dazzling waste ; and soon the bar was crossed,
And the long ridge, where foam for ever tossed
Like fountain sprays around, once past, a mile
Of motionless loveliness without the smile
Of even one young rippling wave stretched on
Till its blue lips the white sand fawned upon.

XI.

Swift in the rowlocks swept the oars, and fast
The boat fled, strained and throbbing, until past
The azure mile, and on the shelving beach
Its brown keel girded sharply ; each to each
Shouted with joyous cries and boyish mirth
To feel beneath their feet the steadfast earth
Again, to see the scared birds scream and fly,
Circling around the waving palms on high,
Heavy with milk-filled nuts, and branches bent
With juicy fruits, and a little stream that sent
Delicious thrills of thirst thro' each one there,
So clear it seem'd, and like some living thing
Dancing and splashing in its wandering ;
And then to feel the very air fill'd full
Of scents delicious stealing from the cool
Green forest shades, heavy magnolias fair
O'er-brimmed with odours sweet, green maiden-hair
Quivering above the intoxicating bliss
Of heavy-laden lilies, each a kiss
Lost to the world of lovers, but grown here
To shape and hue of festooned orchids made
Of colours such as burn in rainbows, fade
Gloriously in sundown western skies,
Or shine within the splendour of sunrise :
Great fragrant blossoms twined amongst the trees
Like prisoned birds of paradise, by bees

And gorgeous insects haunted, and such deeps
Of billowy green, the loveliness that sweeps
The soul more swift to joy than brightest flow'rs,
As though the forest were a myriad bow'rs
Too fair for man, wrought hither into one
For the fair Dreams of old who 'neath the sun
Laugh'd in the vales of Tempe, or outrun
The stag in Attic woods, or danced upon
Hymettus and the slopes of Helicon.

XII.

But one amongst the joyous men withdrew
And wander'd inland, for his spirit knew
That rapt delight in its own subtle mood
When the soul craves and yearns for solitude
Akin to its own loneliness of joy.
A man in strength and stature, yet a boy
In years and heart, to whom the whole sweet, fair,
And beautiful world was a thing laid bare
By God for man to love, to whom it seemed
A loveliness more sweet than he had dreamed
Of woman in the passionate dreams of youth :
He saw the joy and glory, not the ruth
And death and grief that unto older eyes
Dwell likewise there, as water underlies
The still white beauty of the frost : but to
The poet it must seem so ever, new
And fresh and wonderful and sweet and true
And ever-changing, for although he know
The strange coincidence of natural woe
With what to him is as the breath of God,
He sees beyond and deeper—every clod
Of earth that holds a flow'r-root is to him
The casement of a miracle ; in the grim

Reflux, decay, that doth pervade all things,
He sees not but the shadow of death's wings,
But only mists of sleep and change that drift
Till the bowed face of Life again shall lift.

XIII.

As the hot day swooned into afternoon,
Hotter and hotter grew the air, and soon
All the north-western space of sky became
Heavy, metallic, where the heat did flame
In quivering bronze ; and the sea grew changed
Tho' moveless still, as though dark rivers ranged
Purple and green and black throughout its deeps.
At times, as a shudder comes o'er one who sleeps
And dreams of something evil, swiftly flew
Across its face a chill that changed the blue
To a sheet of beaten silver ; then again
It slept on as before, but as in pain.

XIV.

And suddenly the ship's gun fired, and then
Three times the ensign dipped ; startled, the men
A moment stared, then down the shingly strand
Sped swiftly, and from the silvery sand
That edged the wave-line launched their boat, and
    sprang
Each to his place, and soon there sharply rang
Through the electric air the cleaving oars
That swept them seaward from the island shores.

XV.

The sea seemed changed to oil, heavy and dark
And smooth, with frequently a blotch-like mark

Or stain, as though the lifeless waves had died
Of some disease, and lain and putrified.
And like a drop of oil, heavy and thick,
A rain-drop fell, making a sheeny flick
That glitter'd strangely : then another came,
Another, and another, till a flame
Of pale wan light flicker'd above the waves
That slept; or lifeless lay, as over graves
New-made a ghastly glimmer drifts and gleams,
Or as that vagrant fire that faintly streams
O'er lonely marsh-lands thro' each swarthy night.
There was a strange, weird, calm, unearthly light
Shifting about the sky, as o'er the face
Of one who had been fair a smile might chase
The horror of some madness half away.
The raindrops ceas'd : from the boat's oars the spray
Fell heavily : and then once more it rained
Slow drops awhile the boat's crew gained
The ship, where all with waiting, anxious eyes,
Watched the metallic gloom of brazen skies.

XVI.

And suddenly there crashed a dreadful peal
Right overhead—the whole world seemed to reel
And stagger with the blow : the heaven's womb
Opened and brought forth flame : an awful gloom
Stretched like a pall and shrouded up the sun ;
Then once again the thunder seem'd to stun
The shaking firmament, and livid jags
Of lightning tore the cloud-pall into rags.
Again, and yet again as tho' 'twere hurled
Straight down for the destruction of the world,
And yet again like hell's fire uncontrolled :
And ceaselessly the deafening thunder rolled

Above and all around, as though the ship
Was in the hollow of God's hand, whose grip
Would close ere long and into powder grind.
At last burst forth the fury of the wind
Imprison'd long, which like a wild beast sprang
Upon the panting sea, and howling swang
Its great frame to and fro, and yelled and tore
Its heaving breast, tossing thick foam like gore
In savage glee about; and like a spray
Of blossom whirled before a gale, away
The ship was swept o'er boiling seas that fled
Before the wild wind howling as it spread
Far from its thunderous caverns overhead.

XVII.

And not till then it suddenly was known
That on the island whence their bark had flown
One who had thither gone was left behind—
He who had wandered inland : but the wind
Blew ever with a shrill and doleful cry,
Calling the bloodhound waves to faster fly
And seize the fleeing ship; a million deaths
Leagues behind follow'd them with clamorous breaths;
To turn were to perish, and so they sped
Onward, as helpless as a whirling grain
Of sand upon a tempest-stricken plain.

XVIII.

Meanwhile the island trembled 'neath the pow'r
Of the rushing wind, as though its final hour
Had come upon it; but he whose eager eyes
Watched the frail ship being hurl'd far out of sight
Feared not so much himself the tempest's might,

But rather for those friends swept far away.
If saved, he knew that some immediate day
Would see the white sails gleaming on the sea
Beyond the bar again, and joyously
He laughed to think of happy hours to spend
Yet here awhile. Two hours passed, and the end
O' the storm came ; and while he watched it sweep
Like a destroying angel o'er the deep,
Far to the south, the sun shone forth again,
The birds shook from their wings the clinging rain
And thrilled the air with gladness, and the land
Bloomed out afresh, and on the singing sand
The waves broke with a soft repentant motion ;
Miles and miles stretched the foaming, dancing ocean,
Tossing blue waves in glee, and whirling spray
Hither and thither, until tired of play
And wearying for calm dreams it also grew
Quiet and still, and slept in one dense blue.

XIX.

It was now late in the sweet afternoon,
The hours of shadow and sweet rest ; and soon
The day would fall asleep in sunset clouds
And twilight steal and cover earth with shrouds
Of mourning dusk, until the solemn night
Would eastward come crown'd with the lambent light
Of the full golden moon. But still the sun
Hung high in the west, nor would his course be run
For one hour yet or more, and land and sea
Owned him yet lord in regnant majesty.

XX.

On the north-west of the island rose a height,
Crown'd with tall waving palms, of coral white,

Heaved through long years from sea-depths far below,
Thither the young man turned his steps to go
To see the farewell splendours of the day
All marshall'd in magnificent array.

XXI.

He passed whole brakes of sweet magnolias, fair
Orchids with flushed white breasts and streaming hair,
Lilies with languorous golden eyes, and flowers
That stooped to kiss him from their leafy bowers
Hid in green spaces ; then right through a glade
Of trembling tree-ferns wander'd ; then the shade
Of lofty palms enclosed him, till he came
Once more on orchids, each one as a flame,
Scarlet, or white, or purple, tree-ferns high
Warming their trailing tresses 'neath the sky,
Where the sun burn'd low down, frond lay on frond
Of spiked green cacti, and at last, beyond
A stretch of dazzling sand, laughing in glee,
The blue, bright, jubilant waters of the sea.

XXII.

And suddenly he started as though stung
By some hid stake, then down his frame he flung
And looked with eager eyes.   Upon the strand
He saw brown figures move—a joyous band
Of laughing girls: and lo, upon the crown
Of a great billow that came thundering down,
One fair girl-shape, with long hair blown behind,
Poised for a moment !   The soft western wind
Thrill'd with sweet echoed cries, and then once more
A great curved billow swooped upon the shore

Bearing an agile form that gleam'd forth bright
Like shining bronze against the sunset light.

XXIII.

Quite close upon the shore he lay ; so near,
He saw the happy light within their clear
Dark eyes, and saw their joyous laughter make
A sweetness round their lips, and saw them shake
The thick black tresses of their hair, all wet
With salt sea-spray.   He thought that he had met
The fabled sirens, or the nymphs of eld,
Whom Pan loved dearly, by hard fate compell'd
To leave their antique Greece—and as he stood
Wrapt in the pleasant vision of this mood,
A cry shrill'd suddenly along the sand,
And in a moment almost the bare strand
Stretched white and lonely, for as shadows flee
When the sun springs impetuously,
From mountain peak to peak so swiftly fled
The nude bronze figures.   The sinking sun, red
Like a wounded warrior-king, lay down
I' the west to die, taking his shining crown
Of gold from off his brow, which unseen hands
Held poised above him in mid-air : the lands
That he had conquer'd thro' the long fierce day,
And seas that owned his rule, faded away
Before his filming eyes, but, ere the night
Should come, once more he rais'd his stricken sight
From out the purple royal robes that wound
About his limbs—stared straight, as on a hound
Baying a lion far off, on Night whose size
Gigantic loomed i' the east—strove yet to rise
But could not—so lay back with glazing eyes

Upon the blood-stain'd clouds—while overhead
A star leapt forth knowing his lord was dead.

XXIV.

But he had heard that in these happy isles
Friendly the natives were—that welcome smiles
Met each who wander'd there—so forth he went
Across the shingly strand, then stopped and sent ·
A shrill cry through the air, and speedily
Tall lissom figures drew anear; then he
By signs related how the changeful sea
Had brought him thither, and how hunger made
Him weary: and thereafter, when he stayed
His signs and waited, one who seem'd a chief
Stepped forth and handed him a palm-tree leaf,
In sign of friendship, and with kindly eyes
Lifted his hand and waved it all around,
As though to say that all things he had found
Were his, that here he might find welcome rest,
And live with them, partaking of their best.

XXV.

They led him then across the sands to where,
In a delicious hollow where cool air
That late had wander'd on the thirsty seas
Dwelt in green spaces, 'neath great branchéd trees
Cluster'd their huts : and entering into one
The old chief led him as an honour'd son,
And soon sweet fruits and flesh of fowl and kid
Were laid before him, plantain bread amid
Its broad green leaves, and the strong native wine
The palm-nuts give, and sweet fish from the brine

New caught, and water from a running stream
That gurgled near like music in a dream.

XXVI.

The short and tender twilight had now fled,
And all night's starry hosts shone overhead
In myriad fires, and rising suddenly
The orb'd and yellow moon above the sea
Shone full : it might have been the risen soul
From a dead sea whose waves had ceased to roll.

XXVII.

And at the sound of laughter on the sands
Those in the hut came forth : clapping his hands,
The old chief made shrill summons, and anear
One drew—a living loveliness, with clear,
Dark wonderful eyes whose depths contained
The passionate spirit in the flesh enchained :
A mouth like some wild rosebud red, a bare
Bronzed beautiful neck, round which her waving hair
Swayed like the wind-blown tendrils of a vine,
Or like the tangled sea-weed in the brine
Tide-drifted to and fro; her bosom swelled,
Urged by her panting heart, as when beheld
Of old the queen, whose face made all the world
One war, the eyes of Anthony—or as
When Helen flush'd when Paris first did pass
Before her with fixt gaze; around her waist
A girdle of fair feathers interlaced
With cowrie shells drooped slant-wise to her knee
And small and delicate feet ; like those that flee
Among the shadowy hills at dawn when far
The twilight-hours speed 'fore the morning star,

Press'd but scarce marked the sand, she stood as one
Tranced in a vision, and he as on that sun
Columbus stared that offered him the West.
Love's fire was litten sudden in each breast.

XXVIII.

Ah, in the years to come how that night seemed
Some beautiful vision that he long since dreamed!
The moon rose slowly o'er the sea, as though
She linger'd in those heavenly ways wherethro'
The stars shone as bright flowers ; the leagueless deep
Had lullabied its waters into sleep,
And only at long intervals there blew
A cool, soft fanning wind that ere long grew
Aweary also, and so stirred aside,
The slow reluctant leaves, and like a tide
Crept ever farther in amongst the trees
Till in a little dell, with flow'rs the bees
Haunted all day, it sank to restful ease.
Laughter and wild strange music from curv'd shells
And palm-tree flute far echoed ; the sea swell
Urged hushfully into endless monotone—
And he the ship had left stood there alone
And knew it not, for his whole life was filled
With the utter peace, and his spirit thrilled
With imminent joy, and all his heart was hot
With new-born love, and all else was forgot.

XXIX.

When he that night lay sleeping on his bed,
Woven of palm-tree fibre, strange dreams fled
Like ghosts through the dark valley of his sleep.
He dreamt he saw the green weeds of the deep

Swaying unconscious of the light of day,
And 'neath their convolutions lo ! there lay
Two shining gems that seem'd alike with light :
And then he dreamt that dark eternal night
Brooded for ever, without change, around—
Till suddenly two stars leapt with a bound
From out the womb of chaos, staring straight
Upon him : and next he dreamed that fate
Had wash'd his wandrown'd body to the strand
Where the waves wanton'd with him, when a hand
He saw not pulled him from the brine that made
His tangled hair like sea-weed, softly laid
His wave-tossed head upon a bank of flowers, and drew
A palm branch 'twixt him and the burning blue
Of heaven ; and then he oped his weary eyes
And met the gaze of one from Paradise :
And then he woke, and knew the gems he saw
Down in the ocean's depths with such strange awe,
And the two stars that made th' eternal night
Pregnant with message, and the orbs that o'er
Him bent when death had washed him to the shore,
Where each time but the eyes of her whose gaze
Had flashed to his soul's utmost depths, whose face
Seemed burned and printed in his heart : whose grace
Haunted his inward vision as when floats
The fair mirage 'fore him who far off notes
Its unsubstantial beauty, shining clear,
Yet never to be reached or be brought near.

xxx.

Six days passed, and it seem'd as though he had
Dwelt there since birth : joyous, unthinking, glad,
He was at one with those who lived around.
They called him by some sweet name like a sound

Of distant music, and the name that meant
So much to him, and all the quick blood sent
Up to her face whene'er to her he spake
Was Aluhá.   Oft by a little lake
That inland lay half hidden by great white
And scented lilies, curtain'd from the light
By tall and shadowy fronds of fern, they strolled
Hand claspt in hand ; and when the fragrant gold
That was the heart of some great forest-flow'r
Fell on their face and hands in a sudden show'r,
Stirred by some quivering wing of bird the heat
Kept silent 'midst the leaves, her laughter sweet
Rippled like falling water, till their eyes
Of a sudden met, and a swift flush did rise
And make her face a ruddy damask rose,
And his hand trembled as of one who knows
A perilous abyss beside him yawn.
And in the tender beauty of the dawn
Together they went down and watched the sea
With little wavelets splashing hushfully
Beyond the breaking rollers, till afar
The east was seen to tremble, and a star
Made of pure gold to twinkle on a wave,
Till suddenly the sun, as from a grave
A soul might spring rejoicing, sprang sheer up
Above the sky-line—and as from a cup
O'er brimm'd the flooded water pours, clear gold
Along the lifted waves resistless rolled.

XXXI.

And on the seventh day the tropic sun
Grew fiercer still; the noon heats seemed to stun
Both sea and land, and the long afternoon
Lay like a furnace on the deep : the moon

Sailed through the breathless sky at last and brought
Cool shadows ; till a little breeze long sought
Wander'd on vagrant wings unto the isle.
Where the strand crescent curv'd, almost a mile
From the palm-shaded huts, there was a bend
Of forest, sweet with heavy scents, the end
Of a magnolia brake ; and overhead
Tall treeferns waved, and thick grass made a bed
Whence the dark sky and stars were seen alone,
And the sea was not save for its hush'd moan.

XXXII.

And there the lovers lay silent and still.
At times the listless wind would send a thrill
Through the dark leaves, or a hidden bird would shake
Its wings while dreaming, or a wave would break
On the unseen sea with an unusual sound,
Or suddenly a beetle on the ground
Would clang its sharded wings, yet these but made
The silence deeper.   Lost within the shade
The lovers lay ; her dark eyes watched a star
Straining in heaven as though its fires impelled
It forth to spring where it far down beheld
The earth in soft light spin ; he watched her eyes
Reflect the painting star-fire in the skies ;
And then he trembled and once strove to speak,
But could not.   Then against his flushing cheek
A tress of hair wind-lifted from her breast
Brushed gently, then he sudden stooped and pressed
His lips to hers, and clasped her close and cried,
In a strange voice, *Aluhá !*   Side by side
Slient they lay awhile, as though half dazed
By extreme passion : till at last she raised
Her eyes to his with one long look that thrilled
His spirit with love's ecstasy fulfilled.

XXXIII.

And like a dream the long night drifted past ;
As a thick mist, stirred by no mountain blast
But moving in some strange mysterious way,
Drifts o'er the steep hill-sides.   Faint, wan, and grey
The far east grew, and in the dusky sky
The moon sail'd lustreless, and mistily
The planets shone, and paled each starry fire,
Each like some sad and unfulfilled desire.

XXXIV.

And when the sun rose it was in a mist
Wrought of pale gold, purple, and amethyst,
Changing to lovely carmine, then to rose,
Then to a faint blue haze of heat ; like snows
That melt away before the soft south wind
Each wandering cloud faded the sun behind :
And over all the quivering sky there spread
A deepening haze, so that overhead
The sun, tho' flaming fiercely, was not seen.
Ere this the light stirred through the leafy screen,
And woke the lovers : In his eyes the fire
Of passion was not quenched, and still desire
Dwelt in the shadowy depths of those he loved :
Still hand in hand they lay ; and neither moved,
As though they feared the breaking of some charm
Too dear for speech.   At last she stole her arm
Around his neck, and put her lips to his
And wedded him again with one long kiss—
And all the blood within him was like wine
Burning his veins ; his spirit felt divine
In the first flush of love surpassing sweet,
And in this climax life seem'd made complete.

XXXV.

Then hand in hand, with ever and again
Eyes seeking eyes, as though with hungry pain
Love starved for reassurance, ever new
And wonderful,—they went, shaking the dew
That glistened on each leaflet, to the ground.
There was an ominous absence of all sound,
Such as most mornings knew ; the quivering haze
Curtain'd the well-lov'd sky, and to their gaze
It seemed the palms and heavy flowers stooped
Already heavy, and in the shadow drooped
The birds with half-closed wings, or swiftly sped
Voiceless to deeper shade : but overhead
A whirling insect flew with a fierce drone
Shrill and metallic : with a stifled moan
The brooding sea remembered some old grief.
And when upon the ground a wither'd leaf
Fell rustling, though not a breath of wind blew there,
It whirled in circles thro' the electric air.

XXXVI.

Aluhá passed into her hut, and he
Sought coolness in his own : noon heavily
Drew near, and with a brooding sense of pain,
Fill'd up the day. All nature seem'd to strain
Expectant of some evil, as men wait
Helpless the heavy hand of imminent fate.

XXXVII.

And suddenly like some far-distant gun
A long low rumble mutter'd : the red sun
Shrank thro' a livid mist, and shone no more.
A billowy swell swept swiftly on the shore,

Though no wind blew ; the oily sea was freaked
With lines such as a stagnant pool is streaked ;
And the tall palm trees shiver'd, as a breath
Of icy air had whispered them of death.

XXXVIII.

Again, like far artillery in the sky,
The distant thunder rattled ; a low sigh
Moan'd o'er the deep, but not a drop of rain
Fell from above,—then all was still again.
Dark and more dark it grew, as though the day
Were shadow'd in eclipse ; but far away
Strange sudden lights were darting through the clouds,
Like gleaming corpse lights o'er a dead sun's shrouds ;
And darker still it grew, till overhead
A terrible livid blackness was outspread,
And the storm brooded right above the isle.
Still the same awful silence ! mile on mile
Of wan and purply waters lay as tho'
They sank from some fierce scourge, and to and fro
A surface-current twisted like a black
And sinuous serpent ; the salt sea-wrack
Oozed out a filthy scum that sullenly
Blotched the dead calm with spots like leprosy.

XXXIX.

And suddenly, as 'twere the crash of doom,
Heaven seem'd to rock ! from out the blasted womb
Of the thick darkness belched a stream of fire
Blazing and burning, as though hell's desire
Furrowed the world, that shook and quaked and reeled
As deafeningly the dreadful thunder pealed

From horrible abysses in the sky.
And in the midst thereof a piercing cry
Of human pain followed a livid flash
Of lightning, when again a dreadful crash
Blasted the air o'erhead while rock and steep
Shook as by motion of the swaying deep.

XL.

Then, as though all the floods that heav'n had stored
For days and days were loose, the dense rain poured
Downward in blinding torrents : till an hour
Dragged slowly past ; and then it seem'd the power
O' the storm had vanish'd. Far off in the east
The thunder howled still, like a savage beast
Famished and tearing at its stricken prey.
But from the isle it was now far away,
And the sun shone once more, and a cool breeze
Blew from the south, and the drench'd dripping trees
Flashed as though clad in shining coats of mail.
And lo ! upon the west sea-marge a sail
Hover'd like some white bird,—but heeding not
The sea or what it held, the lover sought
His bride of one sweet night, and drawing near,
Called *Aluhà !* And then with sudden fear
He saw her father's hut was torn half down,
And part all scarred and scorched ; its crown
Of palm leaves was no more, but on the ground
Lay strewn and broken ; and not a single sound
Bless'd his strained ear. With shaking hands he drew
The fallen leaves aside, and then he knew
Whose dreadful cry it was that shook the air
Above the din ! With all her lovely hair
Strewn o'er the delicate bosom's dusky grey,
And with closed eyes, hence loveless, quiet she lay,

Only adown the tender brow there ran
A narrow furrow.   Close by lay a man,
Her brother, with a scorch'd and blacken'd cheek,
And on his face the unenfranchised shriek
Which swift death intercepted : without stain
Or mark dead also the old chief !   All pain
Was over for them, and their little life
Was ended as a dream or bygone strife.

XLI.

So still they lay : he could not quite believe
Each spark of life had fled.   Could cruel fate weave
Such sorrow from her loom for no good end ?
But when he took the hand which used to send
Such tremors through him, kissing it again
And yet again, and felt the dreadful pain
Of no response, and in a numbed strange daze,
Looked in the eyes where from his eager gaze
Death shrouded up the soul, he knew at last
All that had come to him : his sweet dream past,
His passionate love a thing that was no more,
But only a stinging memory to brood o'er ;
Life turned a little wearier, and the morn
Of youth grief-clouded, older grown, forlorn—
When all this came upon him the sobs shook
His strong young frame.   And then once more he took
His dear love in his arms, and kissed her lips
As through her spirit yet from the eclipse
Wherein it lay might wake—calling her wife
And darling, his dear love, his joy, his life,
Till the sobs choked his utterance and stayed
The agony of his loss.   And then he laid
Her gently down, and one long farewell gazed,
Then left and wander'd forth as one half-dazed.

XLII.

'Twas late in the afternoon when down the strand
He saw one running towards him with his hand
Pointing out seaward o'er the curving bay,
And lo ! before his eyes his own ship lay
With yards squared round, and urged by splashing oars
The long boat steering for the island shores.

XLIII.

A few short hours ago he would have bid
The old life glad good-bye, choosing amid
The island folk to dwell—but now the land
Was hateful to him, for no loving hand
Would beckon him again by the little lake
That slumber'd lily-clad ; no eye would make
His heart beat fast with joy ; and never again
Would the dear voice replace the last hour's pain.

XLIV.

So when the boat's keel grided on the shore,
And eager shipmates clasped his hand once more,
A great weight was uplifted from his heart :
Yet was he loth when the hour came to part
With those who loved him and had made him seem
One of themselves.   But soon 'twas all a dream,
Strange and unreal, when, standing on the deck,
He saw the island lessen to a speck
In the fast gathering twilight.   Soon his eyes
No more beheld the earthly paradise
Where he had tasted the sweet joy of love,
Yet the same solemn moon that sailed above
Had seen their passion bloom, a tropic flower,
Through one delicious, lost, remember'd hour.

THE CORROBOREE.

XLV.

For youth is but a glad forgetfulness,
Or rather passing onward : the years bless
With such sweet copious gifts, the soul stays not
To linger with sad sorrows best forgot ;
But like the tender south wind of the spring
And the blue skies are fair : what good to wait
By this or that blown rose until too late
We find the sombre autumn drawing nigh
Wherein few roses bloom ? For steadily
The years come round wherein past youth doth seem
The irrevocable beauty of a dream.

1880.   *William Sharp.*

THE CORROBOREE.—(MIDNIGHT.)

DEEP in the forest-depths the tribe
   A mighty blazing fire have made :
. Round this they spring with frantic yells
   In hideous pigments all arrayed—

One barred with yellow ochre, one
   A skeleton in startling white,
Then one who dances furiously
   Blood-red against the great fire's light,—

With death's insignia on his breast,
   In rude design, the swart chief springs ;
And loud and long each echoes back
   The savage war-cry that he sings.

Within the forest dark and dim
  The startled cockatoos like ghosts
Flit to and fro, the mopokes scream,
  And parrots rise in chattering hosts;

The gins and lubras crouch and watch
  With eager, shining, brute-like eyes,
And ever and again shrill back
  Wild echoes of the frantic cries :—

Like some infernal scene it is—
  The forest dark, the blazing fire,
The ghostly birds, the dancing fiends,
  Whose savage chant swells ever higher.

Afar away gaunt wild-dogs howl,
  And strange cries vaguely call : but white
The placid moon sails on, and flame
  The silent stars above the night.

William Sharp.

SNOWY RIVER, NEW SOUTH WALES,
  March 1877.

CHRISTOPHE.

" KING HENRI is King Stephen's peer,
  His breeches cost him but a crown ! "
So from the old world came the jeer
  Of them that hunted Toussaint down :

But what was he,—this slave that swept
The shambles, then to greatness leapt?
Their counterfeit in bronze, a thing
To mock,—or every inch a king?

On Sans Souci's defiant wall
    His people saw against the sky,
Christophe,—a shape the height of Saul,—
    A chief who brooked no rivals nigh.
Right well he aped the antique state,
His birth was mean, his heart was great;
No azure filled his veins,—instead,
The Afric torrent, hot and red.

He built far up the mountain-side
    A royal keep, and walled it round
With towers the palm-tops could not hide;
    The ramparts toward ocean frowned;
Beneath, within the rock-hewn hold,
He heaped a monarch's store of gold,
He made his nobles in a breath;
He held the power of life and death;

And here through torrid years he ruled
    The Haytian horde, a despot king,—
Mocked Europe's pomp,—her minions schooled
    In trade and war and parleying,—
Yet reared his dusky heirs in vain:
To end the drama, Fate grew fain,—
Uprose a rebel tide, and flowed
Close to the threshold where he strode.

" And now the Black must exit make,
  A craven at the last," they say :
Not so,—Christophe his leave will take
  The long unwonted Roman way.
" Ho I ho I " cried he, " the day is done,
And I go down with the tropic sun I "
A pistol-shot—no sign of fear,—
So died Christophe without a peer.

Edmund Clarence Stedman.

THE SLEDGE AT THE GATE.

I WOULD run this arrow straight into my heart
  Sooner than see what I saw to-night.
I harnessed my reindeer, mounted the sledge,
  And examined the snow by the northern light.
The thin ice crackled, the water roared,
            But I crossed the fiord ;
I reach the house when the night is late,
What's this ?   A deer and a sledge at the gate !

O the eyes of Zela are winter springs I
  But the wealth of summer is in her hair ;
But she loves me not, she is false again,
  Or why are the sledge and the reindeer there ?
I throw myself down, face-first in the snow ;
            " *Let the false one go I* "
She never shall know my love, or my scorn,
For I shall be frozen stiff in the morn.

The sharp winds blew, and my limbs grew chill.
  I knew no more till I felt the fire.

They rubbed my breast, and they rubbed my hands,
  And my life came back like a dark desire.
She spake kind words, and smoothed my hair,
        But the sledge was there !
" Oh false, but fair !" It was all I said,
I struck her down, and away I fled.

I mounted my sledge, and the reindeer flew,
  In the wind, in the snow, in the blinding sleet :
The snow was heavy, the wind like a knife,
  And the ice like water under my feet.
The wolves were hungry—they scented my track—
        But I fought them back !
·I fear neither wolves, nor the winter's cold,
For the faithless woman has made me bold.

2

· *" Yes, we are merry Cossacks."*

Yes, we are merry Cossacks,
  Though not the Russian breed ;
But bring a steed from Ilmen,
  And fatten the lean steed.

When we come back with plunder,
  We are true Cossacks then :
We sleep in the arms of beauties,
  My merry, merry men.

3

" He rode from the Khora Tukhan."

He rode from the Khora Tukhan
  On his nimble bay steed,
For the eyes of his mistress, Girgalla,
  Forsaking his creed.

He gave his broad belt to his comrade.
  Why scoff you ? he said.
The sheep are all killed for the wedding,
  The dishes are spread.

I have sat in the rains and the thunders,
  Alone since she went.
I would I could sit down beside her,
  Beneath the white tent !

When I lift to my lips the red tea-cup,
  Slow sipping the tea,
I think of the lips of Girgalla,
  And sigh, " Woe is me ! "

I peeped through the snowy tent curtains,
  Girgalla was there :
She stood like a peacock before me,
  No peacock so fair.

Your head on the lap of Girgalla,
  Stretched out at your ease,
No cushion, you say, of swan's feathers
  So soft as her knees !

4.
" Forgive me, mother dear."

Forgive me, mother dear,
  For the days of unrest
And the sleepless nights you passed
  When I sucked from your breast.

Dig my grave on a hill,
  On the summit let it stand,
That the wind may blow my dust
  To my own Tartar land.

                    Richard Henry Stoddard.

FRIDTHJOF AT SEA.

I.

BUT, wood and afeard
  Helge stood on the shore,
To the goblin so weird
  Dark spells mutt'ring o'er.

See ! heav'n's vault now clouds are treading ;
  Crashing thunders Ran's wastes sweep.
Fast her boiling waves are spreading,
  Sparkling froth o'er all the deep.
See ! i' th' sky red lightning's fasten
  Here and there a bloody band ;
Ocean's sea-birds, frighten'd, hasten,
  Harshly screaming, to the strand,—

  " Desp'rate weather, comrades !
  Hark ! the storm, I hear a-
  Far his pinions flapping,—
  But we grow not pale :
  Sit in peace with Balder,
  Think of me and long !— Oh,
  Beauteous in thy sorrow,
  Beauteous Ingeborg ! "

II.

'Gainst Ellide came
  Of trolls a grim pair ;
'Twas the wind-cold Ham,
  'Twas Hejd with snow-hair.

Then the storm unfetter'd wingeth
  Wild his course ; in ocean's foam
Now he dips him, now up-swingeth,
  Whirling toward the god's own home :

Rides this horror-spirit, warning,
   High upon the topmost wave—
Up from out the white, vast, yawning,
   Bottomless, unfathom'd grave.

   " Fairer was our voyage,
   Moonlight glitt'ring round us,
   O'er the mirroring billows
   Hence to Balder's grove :
   Warmer than 'tis here, my
   Ing'borg's heart was beating,—
   Whiter than the sea-foam
   Swell'd her bosom then ! "

                III.

   Now, Solund's Isles see
      'Mong white breakers stand ;—
   There all calm the waves will be,
      There's your port, steer to land !

But the dauntless Viking fears not
   On his true-fast oak so soon ;
Hard the helm he grasps and hears not,
   But with joy winds sport aboon.
Tighter still the sail he stretches,
   Faster still he cuts his way,—
Westward, west, due west, he fetches,
   Rush the billow as it may !

   " Fain one moment longer
   Fierce I'd fight the tempest ;
   Storms and Norsemen flourish
   Well together here.

For a gust to landward,
Should her ocean-eagle,
Fearful, feebly flutter—
How would Ing'borg blush !"

IV.

But each wave's now a hill,
    Down yet deeper they reel,
Blasts in cordage sing shrill,—
    Strains the grating keel :

Yet howe'er the surges wrestle,
    Whether for or 'gainst they rise,—
Still Ellide, god-built vessel,
    All their angry threats defies ;
Like some star-shoot in the gloaming,
    Glad she bounds along and leaps
Goat-like o'er rough mountains roaming,
    Now o'er heights and now o'er deeps !

    " Better felt soft kisses
    From my bride with Balder,
    Than, as here I stand, to
    Taste this up-thrown brine.
    Better 'twas t' encircle
    Ing'borg's waist so slender,
    Than, as here, tight-clasping
    This hard rudder bar !"

V.

But the snow big cloud
    Icy knife-gusts pours ;
And on deck, shield, shroud,
    Clatter hailstone showers ;

And from stem to stern on board her,
  Naught thou canst for night descry,
Dark 'tis there, as in that chamber
  Where the dead imprisoned lie.
Down 'mid whirlpool-horror dashes
  Th' implacable bedevil'd wave ;
While grey-white, as strown with ashes,
  Gapes one endless, soundless grave.

     " Ran our beds of blue is
     Spreading 'mong the billows,
     But for me is waiting
     Thy bed, Ingeborg !
     Yes ! stout-hearted fellows,
     Lift thy oars, Ellide,
     Gods thy good keel builded,—
     Yet awhile we'll swim !"

               VI.

     O'er the starboard broke
       Now a mountain-sea,
     And with whelming stroke
       Swept her deck all free.

Fridthjof then his armlet taking
  (Three marks weigh'd it, and was old
Bele's gift, nor morn's awaking
  Sun outshone in fine-wrought gold),
Quick the dwarf-carv'd ring in pieces
  Hews relentless with his sword,
And, the fragments sharing, misses
  None of all his line on board.

     " Gold, on sweetheart ramblings,
     Pow'rful is and pleasant ;

Who goes empty-handed
Down to sea-blue Ran,
Cold her kisses strike, and
Fleeting her embrace is—
But we, ocean's bride be-
Troth with purest gold ! "

VII.

Threat'ning still his worst,
    Roars the storm again ;
Quick the sheet is burst,
    Snaps the yard in twain.

'Gainst th' half-buried ship, commotion-
Toss'd high waves to boarding go ;
And howe'er they bale, is ocean
Not so soon bal'd out, we know !
Not e'en Fridthjof now doubts longer
That he carries death on board ;
Yet than storm or billow stronger,
Higher sounds his lordly word.

" Hither Bjorn ! the rudder
Grasp with bear-paw strongly ;
Valhal's pow'rs sure send not
Weather such as this ;
Witchcraft's workings ! Helge,
Coward-scoundrel, doubtless
Conjured has these billows,—
I will up and see ! "

VIII.

Like marten he flew
    Up the bending mast ;
And there, fast-clinging, threw
    Many a glance on the waste.

Look ! as isle that loose-torn drifteth,
    Stops that whale Ellide's way ;
Sea-fiends two the monster lifteth
    High on's back, through boiling spray ;
Hejd is wrapp'd in snowy cov'ring,
    Fashion'd like the white-furr'd bear,—
Ham, 'mid whistling winds, grim, hov'ring,
    Storm-bird-like assaults the air.

" Now, Ellide ! show us
Whether, as 'tis boasted,
Hero-mood thy iron-fast
Round oak-bosom holds !
Listen ! art thou truly
Aeger's god-sprung daughter,
Up with copper-keel, and
Gore that spell-charm'd whale ! "

IX.

And Ellide hears
    Her young lord's behest,—
With one bound gulf clears
    To the troll-whale's breast.

From the wound a stream out-gushes,
    Up toward heav'n, of smoking blood ;
And, gashed through, the beast down-rushes,
    Roaring, to the deepest mud ;
Then, at once, the hero slingeth
    Two sharp spears ; one the ice-bear's hide
Pierceth, the other deadly springeth
    Through yon pitch-black eagle's side.

" Bravely struck, Ellide !
Not so soon will Helge's

Dragon-ship leap upward
Out from bloody mud ;
Hejd nor Ham much longer
The up-toss'd sea will keep, for
Bitter 'tis to bite the
Hard blue-shining steel."

X.

And the storm—it had fled
   At once from the sea ;
Only ground-swells led
   To the isle on their lea.

And at once the sun fresh treadeth,
   Monarch-like, in hall of blue ;
Joy o'er ship and wave he spreadeth,
   Hill and dale creates anew.
Sunset's beamings crown with gold the
   Craggy rock and grove-dark plain ;
All with glad surprise behold the
   Shores of Efjesund again.

" Ing'borg's prayers—pale maidens
Up to Valhal rising—
Lily-white, on heav'n's own
Gold-floors bent the knee ;
Tears in light-blue eyes, and
Sighs from swan-down bosoms,
Th' asas' stern hearts melted,—
Thank, then, thank the gods !"

XI.

But Ellide rose
   Sore jarred by the whale,
And water-logg'd goes,
   All awear'd by her sail.

Yet more wearied than their dragon,
  Totter Fridthjof's gallant men ;
Though each leans upon his weapon,
  Scarcely upright stand they then.
Bjorn on powerful shoulder dareth
  Four to carry to the land ;
Fridthjof, all alone, eight bareth—
  Sets them so sound th' upblaz'd brand.

  " Nay, ye white-faced, shame not !
  Waves are mighty Vikings ;
  Hard's th' unequal struggle—
  Ocean's maids our foes.
  See I there comes the mead-horn,
  Wand'ring on bright gold-foot ;
  Shipmates, cold limbs warm, and—
  Here's to Ingeborg I "

Tegnèr (translated by Professor Stephens)

BALDER'S PYRE.

MIDNIGHT'S sun, all blood-red bright,
  Far-off hills o'erbended ;
It was not day, it was not night,
  Between them 'twas suspended.

Balder's pyre, of the sun a mark,
  Holy hearth red staineth ;
Yet soon dies its last faint spark,
  Darkly then Hoder reigneth.

Ancient priests around the temple-wall
  Stood, and the pile-brands shifted ;
Silver-bearded and pale, they all
  Flint-knives in hard hands lifted.

Helge, crown'd standeth them beside,
  Help 'mid the circle proff'ring.
Hark ! then clatter, at midnight's tide,
  Arms in the grove of off'ring.

" Bjorn, the door hold close, man—so !
  Pris'ners they'll all obey me ;
Out or in whoe'er would go,
  Cleave his skull, I pray thee."

Pale waxeth Helge,—that voice too well
  Knows he, and what presaging.
Forth trod Fridthjof, and dark words fell
  Storm-like in autumn raging.

" Here's the tribute, prince, thy breath
  Ordered from western waters ;
Take it, then, for life or death
  Fight we at Balder's altars !

" Back shield-covered, my bosom bare,
  Nought shall unfair be reckon'd,
First, as king, strike thou !   Beware,
  Mind, for I strike the second.

" Yonder door !—nay, gaze, fool, here !
  Caught in his hole the fox is ;
Think of Framness and Ing'borg dear,
  Fam'd that for golden locks is ! "

So his hero-accents rang ;
  Th' purse from his belt then freely
Drew he, and careless enough it flang
  Right at the son of Bele.

Blood from his mouth gush'd out straightway,
  Streaming blackly splendent ;
There by his altar swooning lay
  Th' asas' high descendant.

"What ! thine own gold bear'st not?—shame !
  Shame ! coward-king, vile-shrinking ;
Angesvadil none e'er shall blame
  Blood so base for drinking !

"Silence ! priests with off'ring-knife,
  Chiefs, yon moon lights dimly !
Noise might cost each wretched life ;
  Back !—for my blade thirsts grimly.

"Rageful thine eye, white Balder, shines;
  Yet, why so anger-swollen?
Yon fair ring thine arm round-twines,—
  Pardon me, but 'tis stolen !

"Not sure for thee, Volund, smith kept
  Graving that jewel's wonders !
Violence stole, and the virgin wept.
  Down with all scoundrel plunders ! "

Brave he pull'd ; but fast-grown seem'd
  Th' arm and the ring so curious ;
When loos'd at last, where th' altar gleam'd
  Brightest the god leapt furious.

Hark, that crash ! Gnawing gold-toothed flame
  Rafter and roof o'er quivers ;
Bjorn turns pale as he stands, and shame !
  Fridthjof feels that he shivers.

"Bjorn, release them !   Unbar the door,
    Guarding is now all over :   •
Th' temple blazes; pour water, pour
    All the sea thereover ! "

Now from temple and grove and strand
    Chain-like, they clasp each other ;
Billows, wandering from hand to hand,
    Hissing the fires would smother.

Rain-god-like sits Fridthjof there,
    High o'er beams and waters,
All directing with lordly air,
    Calm 'mong the hot fire-slaughters.

Vain !   Fire conquers ; rolling past
    Smoke-clouds whirl, and smelted
Gold on red-hot sands falls fast,—
    Silver plates are melted.

All, all's lost !   From half-burn'd hall
    Th' fire-red cock up-swingeth,—
Sits on the roof, and, with shrilly call
    Flutt'ring, free course wingeth.

Morning's winds from the north rush by,
    Heav'nward the fire-wave surges ;
Balder's grove is summer dry,
    Greedy the fierce blaze gorges.

Raging from branch to branch it flew,
    Still round the goal ne'er closing ;
Ah ! how fearful that wild light grew,
    Balder's pyre, how imposing !

Hark ! how it snaps i' th' gaping root ;
　See ! from the top sparks shower ;
'Gainst Muspel's sons, the red, what boot
　Man's art, man's arm, man's power ?

Fire-seas tumble in Balder's grove ;
　Shortless the billows wander ;
Sun-beam rise, but frith and cove
　Mirror hell's flame-lights yonder !

T' ashes soon is the temple burn'd,
　T' ashes the grove is blooming ;
Fridthjof, grief-full, away has turn'd,
　Day o'er his hot tears glooming.

Tegnèr.

THE ELECTION TO THE KINGDOM.

To Thing, away o'er dale and hill
　The fire-cross speeds ;
King Ring is dead,—his throne to fill
　A diet need.

To his wall-hung sword each yeoman flies
　Its steel is blue,—
And quick its edge his finger tries,
　It bites right true.

On shine, so steel-blue, joyful gaze
　His laughing boys ;
The blade's too big for one to raise,
　It *two* employs.

From spot and stain his daughter frees
  The helm with care ;
But how she blushes, when she sees
  Her image there !

His shield's round fence, a sun in blood,
  Last guards his mail.
Hail, iron-limbed freeman ! warrior good !
  Hail, yeoman, hail !

Thy country's honour, glory, all,
  Thee gone, would cease ;
In battle still thy brave land's wall,
  Its voice in peace !

Thus gather they, with clang of shields
  And arms' hoarse sound,
In open Thing,—for heav'n's blue field
  Sole roof them around.

But, standing on the Thing-stone there,
  See Fridthjof hold
(A child as yet) the king's young heir,
  With locks of gold.

" Too young's that prince," loud murmur then
  The assembled throng ;
" Nor judge he'll be among his men,
  Nor war-chief strong."

But Fridthjof on his shield lifts high
  The son of Ring ;—
" Northmen ! nor yet your land's hopes die,—
  See here your king !

" See here old Odin's awful race
  In image bright ;
The shield he treads with youthful grace,—
  So fish swims light.

" I swear his kingdom to protect
  With sword and spear ;
Till, with his father's gold-wreath deck'd,
  I crown him here !

" Forsete, Balder's high-born son,
  Hath heard mine oath ;
Strike dead, Forset', if e'er I'm won
  To break my troth ! "

But thron'd king-like, the lad sat proud
  On shield-floor high ;
So the eaglet glad, from rock-hung cloud,
  The sun will eye !

At length this place his young blood found
  Too dull to keep ;
And, with one spring, he gains the ground,
  A royal leap !

Then rose loud shouts from all the Thing,—
  " We, Northmen free,
Elect thee—shield-borne youth ! like Ring,
  Thy father, be !

" 'Neath Fridthjof's guardian counsels live,—
  Thy realm his care ;
Jarl Fridthjof, as thy bride we give
  His mother fair ! "

" To-day," the frowning chief replied,
  " A king we choose,—
Not marry; when I take my bride,
  None for me woos.

" To Balder's sacred grove I go;
  The norns, I dread,
I swore should there be met,—and know
  They wait my tread.

" Yes, all my fortunes, all my love,
  I them will tell ;
Time's spreading tree beneath, above,
  Those shield-maids dwell.

" Balder's, the light-hair'd pale god's wrath
  Still 'gainst me burns ;
None else my heart's young spouse ta'en hath,
  None else returns.'

His brow slight kissing, Ring's fair child
  Salutes he low ;
Then, silent, o'er the heath-plain wild
  He vanish'd slow.

Tegnèr.

THE DEATH OF THE WHITE HERON.

[CYPRESS LAKE, FLORIDA.]

I PULLED my boat with even sweep
Across light shoals and eddies deep,

Tracking the currents of the lake
From lettuce raft to weedy brake.

Across a pool death-still and dim
I saw a monster reptile swim,

And caught, far off and quickly gone,
The delicate outlines of a fawn.

Above the marshy islands flew
The green teal and the swift curlew;

The rail and dunlin drew the hem
Of lily-bonnets over them;

I saw the tufted wood-duck pass
Between the wisps of water-grass.

All round the gunwales and across
I draped my boat with Spanish moss,

And, lightly drawn from head to knee,
I hung gay air-plants over me;

Then, lurking like a savage thing
Crouching for a treacherous spring,

I stood in motionless suspense
Among the rushes green and dense.

I kept my bow half-drawn, a shaft
Set straight across the velvet haft.

Alert and vigilant, I stood
Scanning the lake, the sky, the wood.

I heard a murmur soft and sad
From water-weed to lily-pad,

And from the frondous pine did ring
The hammer of the golden-wing.

On old drift logs the bitterns stood·
Dreaming above the silent flood ;

The water-turkey eyed my boat,
The hideous snake-bird coiled its throat,

And birds whose plumage shone like flame,—
Wild things grown suddenly, strangely tame,—

Lit near me ; but I heeded not :
They could not tempt me to a shot.

Grown tired at length, I bent the oars
By grassy brinks and shady shores,

Through labyrinths and mysteries
'Mid dusky cypress stems and knees,

Until I reached a spot I knew,
O'er which each day the herons flew.

I heard a whisper sweet and keen
Flow through the fringe of rushes green,

The water saying some light thing,
The rushes gaily answering.

The wind drew faintly from the south,
Like breath blown from a sleeper's mouth,

And down its current sailing low
Came a lone heron white as snow.

He cleft with grandly spreading wing
The hazy sunshine of the spring ;

Through graceful curves he swept above
The gloomy moss-hung cypress grove ;

Then gliding down a long incline,
He flashed his golden eyes on mine.

Half-turned he poised himself in air,
The prize was great, the mark was fair !

I raised my bow and steadily drew
The silken string until I knew

My trusty arrow's barbéd point
Lay on my left forefinger joint, —

Until I felt the feather seek
My ear, swift-drawn across my cheek :

Then from my fingers leapt the string
With sharp recoil and deadly ring,

Closed by a sibilant sound so shrill
It made the very water thrill, —

Like twenty serpents bound together
Hissed the flying arrow's feather !

A thud, a puff, a feathery ring.
A quick collapse, a quivering, —

A whirl, a headlong downward dash,
A heavy fall, a sullen plash,

And like white foam, or giant flake
Of snow, he lay upon the lake !

And of his death the rail was glad,
Strutting upon a lily-pad ;

The jaunty wood-duck smiled and bowed ;
The belted kingfisher laughed aloud,

Making the solemn bittern stir
Like a half-wakened slumberer ;

And rasping notes of joy were heard
From gallinule and crying bird,

The while with trebled noise did ring
The hammer of the golden-wing !

Maurice Thompson.

THE FAWN.

I LAY close down beside the river,
My bow well strung, well filled my quiver.

The god that dwells among the reeds
Sang sweetly from their tangled bredes.

The soft-tongued water murmured low,
Swinging the flag leaves to and fro.

Beyond the river, fold on fold,
The hills gleamed through a film of gold ;

The feathery osiers waved and shone
Like silver thread in tangles blown.

A bird, fire-winged, with ruby throat
Down the slow, drowsy wind did float,

And drift and flit and stray along,
A very focal flame of song.

A white sand-isle amid the stream
Lay sleeping by its shoals of bream ;

In lilied pools, alert and calm,
Great bass through lucent circles swam ;

And farther, by a rushy brink
A shadowy fawn stole down to drink

Where tall, thin birds unbalanced stood
In sandy shallows of the flood.

And what did I beside the river
With bow well-strung and well-filled quiver ?

I lay quite still with half-closed eyes,
Lapped in a dream of paradise,

Until I heard a bow-cord ring,
And from the reeds an arrow sing.

I knew not of my brother's luck,
If well or ill his shaft had struck ;

But something in his merry shout
Put my sweet summer dream to rout,

And up I sprang, with bow half drawn,
With keen desire to slay the fawn.

But where was it ? Gone like my dream !
I only heard the fish-hawk scream,

And the strong, stripéd bass leap up
Beside the lily's floating cup ;

I only felt the cool wind go
Across my face with steady flow ;

I only saw those thin birds stand
Unbalanced on the river sand,

Low peering at some dappled thing
In the green rushes quivering.

Maurice Thompson.

THE FLIGHT OF THE RED HORSE.

[A DAKOTA LEGEND.]

" MY son, Woneya, I must make
A journey to the Sacred Lake.
Far to the north, 'mid ice and snow,
A long, long way it is I go.
An arrow flying all the night
Would fail to reach it in its flight.
You are my son ; I give to-day
Full leave to all your childish play.

All things are thine ; go where you will,
Save to the Red House on the hill.
Try not its door, turn not the key ;
There death and ruin wait for thee,
But how and why I may not tell,
For there is laid on me a spell,
So all my love must turn to hate,
And no man can escape his fate."

Washaka goes.   In boyish play
The child wears out the summer day ;
He swims the stream, his crafty hook
Draws shining treasure from the brook ;
The chattering squirrel hugs his limb
As the swift arrow grazes him.
But ever, as he played, he said,
"What is there in the House of Red ?"
Go where he would, each pathway still
Led to the Red House on the hill.

At last he stands before the door,
With mystic symbols pictured o'er.
" What could my father mean," he said,
" To keep me from the House of Red ?"
Ah, no ! he will not disobey,
Although the sire is far away ;
And yet, what harm could come of it
For him to see which key would fit ?

And now he tries them, one by one,
Until the last—what has he done ?
Some thoughtless pressure of the lock,
The door flies open with a shock.
Strange tremors run along the ground ;
The world is full of direful sound ;

Strange voices talk ; strange whispers rise ;
Strange portents in the earth and skies
Through the wide door the youth can see
All that there is of mystery.
Before him stood a Horse of Red,
With mane of gold, who sternly said :
" Unhappy boy ! what have you done ?
Washaka now must slay his son."

Struck down with terror and remorse,
The youth falls prone before the horse.
" Oh, help me, help ! " Woneya cries,
With gasping breath and streaming eyes.
" Teach me some way ; show me the path
Where I may flee my father's wrath."
The horse replies : " The wrong is great,
Yet I have pity for thy fate.
One way alone is left to flee,
With perils fraught to thee and me.
I charge thee, on thy life, thy soul,
To yield thee up to my control.
Look neither backward, left, nor right :
Be brave, and yield no place to fright.
Thy father now will try each art
To strike a terror to thy heart ;
But if thy heart begin to quail,
That instant all my strength will fail ;
And if Washaka us o'ertake,
I, too, must perish for thy sake.
Take in thy hand this conjurer's sack.
Away ! away ! Spring to my back ! "

So said, so done. Away they sped.
The dark sky clamored overhead ;
A mighty wind blew from the east,
Which momently its force increased ;

The sun went down, but, through the night,
He holds his tireless, even flight.
No need is there for spur or rein ;
Life is the prize he strives to gain.
But, though the horse flies like the wind,
The father presses hard behind,
And, ere the break of morn appears,
A dreadful voice is in their ears :
"Stop ! stop ! thou traitor, while my knife
Shall quickly end your wretched life."
"Beware ! beware ! Turn not your head !
Be brave ! be brave !" the Red Horse said.
"Put now your hand within the sack ;
What first you find throw quickly back."
Woneya in an instant found
An egg, and tossed it to the ground :
It bursts, it spreads—a wide morass,
Through which the father may not pass :
Fierce lightnings fire Washaka's eyes
As westward still the Red Horse flies.

Long time the father sought, in vain,
Some passage o'er the marsh to gain,
Where long-necked lizards basked or fought,
Where winged dragons ruin wrought,
Where serpents coiled and hissed, whose breath
Rolled up in clouds of fire and death.
At last he throws the magic bone,
Which turns that teeming life to stone ;
And where he picks his careful way,
There are the Bad Lands to this day.

The morn blooms in the eastern sky ;
The day comes on, the noon is nigh ;

The noon is past, the sun is low,
The evening red begins to glow;
But, driven still by sorest need,
Still swift and swifter flies the steed.
Vast, sky-rimmed plains on either side
Begin to turn in circles wide,
While rock, and shrub, and bush within
In dizzy circles spin and spin.
So swift the flight, so hot the race,
The wind blows backward in his face;
But swifter far than any wind
The father presses on behind,
And to their ears is borne the cry
That summons them again to die.
" Beware !   Be brave !   Turn not thy head !
Put in thy hand !" the Red Horse said ;
" The first thing that thy hand shall find,
That take, and quickly hurl behind."

He draws and throws a bit of stone,
When, 'twixt the father and the son,
A range of mountains rears its height
On either hand beyond the sight.
Washaka seeks a pass in vain ;
To left and right, above the plain,
The strong grim rocks confront his eyes,
While westward still the Red Horse flies.
At last he draws his feathered spear
And hurls against the rampart sheer.
So swift it dashes on the rock,
Fire-streams burst outward at the shock,
And where against the cliff he drives,
From base to top it rends and rives ;
A narrow gorge is opened through,
By which Washaka may pursue.
And now the Red Horse knows the need

To lavish all his garnered speed.
His hoof-beats fall like thunder-dints,
And kindle showers of flying flints;
So swift he flies that one afar
Might deem he saw a falling star ;
But swifter still upon his path
Washaka follows in his wrath.
And now that fearful voice again
Comes o'er the horror-shaken plain :
"Stop, wretches, stop !   Behold the flood !
Now shall my knife run red with blood !
Who now can save you from my hate,
And who has ever conquered fate? "

Alas ! what hope is left, and where ?
What refuge now from blank despair?
The end is come, where shall they flee ?
Before them is the open sea.
"Beware ! beware !   Turn not thy head.
Put in thy hand !" the Red Horse said ;
"Just as we reach the ocean shore,
Draw out and quickly hurl before.
Be strong of heart.   Be calm ; be brave ;
The sea is not to be our grave."
Woneya thrusts his hand within,
Draws forth the bead-wrought serpent's skin,
And casts it forth, when lo ! a boat
Upon the gleaming waves afloat !
They gain it with a single leap
That sends it forward on the deep.
The sails are set ; before the breeze
It draws its white trail o'er the seas
In vain the bright blade of the sire
Whirls through the air in rings of fire.
He gains the beach a moment late —
What man has ever conquered fate?

Vain are his curses, vain his prayer ;
The glittering waves are everywhere.

Washaka stoops along the sands,
Uproots a huge cliff with his hands ;
He heaves aloft with tug and strain,
And sends it wheeling o'er the main.
High in the air it rocks and swings,
A moment to the clouds it clings ;
Then, as from lofty mountain-walls,
Like some vast avalanche, it falls.
The sea shrinks, cringing, from the shock
Of that dark, shapeless bulk of rock,
Like some great fragment of a world
From out the stellar spaces hurled.
Like chaff beneath the flail outspread
The waves, and bare the ocean's bed.
One vast wall, sweeping to the west,
Bears on its topmost curving crest
The tiny boat, so feather-light,
Through all that long and fearful night.
At morn they rest, their journey done,
In a fair land beyond the sun ;
And one, with awful rush and roar,
Springs tiger-like against the shore,
Drags down Washaka from the land,
And hides him 'neath the sliding sand.

Still from that coast a slender bar,
Like a long finger, stretching far,
When tides are low, points o'er the wave—
That is Washaka's lonely grave.

H. E. Warner.

SONG OF THE REDWOOD-TREE.

A CALIFORNIA song,
A prophecy and indirection, a thought impalpable to
    breath as air,
A chorus of dryads, fading, departing, or hamadryads
    departing,
A murmuring, fateful, giant voice, out of the earth and
    sky,
Voice of a mighty dying tree in the redwood forest
    dense.

Farewell my brethren,
Farewell O earth and sky, farewell ye neighbouring
    waters,
My time has ended, my term has come.

Along the northern coast,
Just back from the rock-bound shore and the caves,
In the saline air from the sea in the Mendocino country,
With the surge for base and accompaniment low and
    hoarse,
With crackling blows of axes sounding musically driven
    by strong arms,
Riven deep by the sharp tongues of the axes, there in the
    redwood forest dense,
I heard the mighty tree its death-chant chanting.

The choppers heard not, the camp shanties echoed not,
The quick-ear'd teamsters and chain and jack-screw men
    heard not,
As the wood-spirits came from their haunts of a thousand
    years to join the refrain,
But in my soul I plainly heard.

Murmuring out of its myriad leaves,
Down from its lofty top rising two hundred feet high,
Out of its stalwart trunk and limbs, out of its foot-thick
    bark,
That chant of the seasons and time, chant not of the past
    only but the future.

You untold life of me,
And all you venerable and innocent joys,
Perennial hardy life of me with joys 'mid rain and many
    a summer sun,
And the white snows and night and the wild winds;
O the great patient rugged joys, my soul's strong joys
    unreck'd by man,
(For know I bear the soul befitting me, I too have
    consciousness, identity,
And all the rocks and mountains have, and all the earth,)
Joys of the life befitting me and brothers mine,
Our time, our term has come.

Nor yield we mournfully majestic brothers,
We who have grandly fill'd our time;
With Nature's calm content, with tacit huge delight,
We welcome what we wrought for through the past,
And leave the field for them.

For them predicted long,
For a superber race, they too to grandly fill their time,
For them we abdicate, in them ourselves ye forest kings!
In them these skies and airs, these mountain peaks,
    Shasta, Nevadas,
These huge precipitous cliffs, this amplitude, these valleys,
    far Yosemite,
To be in them absorb'd, assimilated.

Then to a loftier strain,
Still prouder, more ecstatic rose the chant,
As if the heirs, the deities of the West,
Joining with master-tongue bore part.

Not wan from Asia's fetishes,
Nor red from Europe's old dynastic slaughter-house,
(Area of murder-plots of thrones, with scent left yet of
wars and scaffolds everywhere,)
But come from Nature's long and harmless throes, peace-
fully builded thence,
These virgin lands, lands of the Western shore,
To the new culminating man, to you, the empire new,
You promis'd long, we pledge, we dedicate.

You occult deep volitions,
You average spiritual manhood, purpose of all, pois'd on
yourself, giving not taking law,
You womanhood divine, mistress and source of all, whence
life and love and aught that comes from light and
love,
You unseen moral essence of all the vast materials of
America (age upon age working in death the same as
life,)
You that, sometimes known, oftener unknown, really
shape and mould the New World, adjusting it to
Time and Space,
You hidden national will lying in your abysms, conceal'd
but ever alert,
You past and present purposes tenaciously pursued, may-be
unconscious of yourselves,
Unswerv'd by all the passing errors, perturbations of the
surface ;
You vital, universal, deathless germs, beneath all creeds,
arts, statutes, literatures,

Here build your homes for good, establish here, these areas
  entire, lands of the Western shore,
We pledge, we dedicate to you.

For man of you, your characteristic race,
Here may be hardy, swift, gigantic grow, here tower
  proportionate of Nature,
Here climb the vast pure spaces unconfined, uncheck'd by
  wall or roof,
Here laugh with storm or sun, here joy, here patiently
  inure,
Here heed himself, unfold himself (not others' formulas
  heed,) here fill his time,
To duly fall, to aid, unreck'd at last,
To disappear, to serve.

Thus on the northern coast,
In the echo of teamsters' calls and the clinking chains,
  and the music of choppers' axes,
The falling trunk and limbs, the crash, the muffled shriek,
  the groan,
Such words combined from the redwood-tree, as of voices
  ecstatic, ancient and rustling,
The century-lasting, unseen dryads, singing, withdrawing,
All their recesses of forests and mountains leaving,
From the Cascade range to the Wahsatch, or Idaho far, or
  Utah,
To the deities of the modern henceforth yielding,
The chorus and indications, the vistas of coming
  humanity, the settlements, features all,
In the Mendocino woods I caught.

II.

The flashing and golden pageant of California,
The sudden and gorgeous drama, the sunny and ample
  lands,

The long and varied stretch from Puget sound to
    Colorado south,
Lands bathed in sweeter, rarer, healthier air, valleys and
    mountain cliffs,
The fields of Nature long prepared and fallow, the silent,
    cyclic chemistry,
The slow and steady ages plodding, the unoccupied
    surface ripening, the rich ores forming beneath :
At last the new arriving, assuming, taking possession,
A swarming and busy race settling and organising
    everywhere,
Ships coming in from the whole round world, and going
    out to the whole world,
To India and China and Australia, and the thousand
    island paradises of the Pacific,
Populous cities, and latest inventions, the steamers on the
    river, the railroads, with many a thrifty farm, with
    machinery,
The wool and wheat and the grape, and diggings of
    yellow gold.

III.

But more in you than these, lands of the Western shore,
(These but the means, the implements, the standing-
    ground,)
I see in you, certain to come, the promise of thousands of
    years, till now deferr'd,
Promis'd to be fulfill'd, our common kind, the race.

The new society at last, proportionate to Nature,
In man of you, more than your mountain peaks or
    stalwart trees imperial,
In woman more, far more, than all your gold or vines, or
    even vital air.

Fresh come, to a new world indeed, yet long prepared,
I see the genius of the modern, child of the real and
    ideal,
Clearing the ground for broad humanity, the true
    America, heir of the past so grand,
To build a grander future.

Walt Whitman.

FROM FAR DAKOTA'S CANONS.

FROM far Dakota's canons,
Lands of the wild ravine, the dusky Sioux, the lonesome
    stretch, the silence,
Haply to-day a mournful wail, haply a trumpet note for
    heroes.

The battle-bulletin,
The Indian ambuscade, the craft, the fatal environment,
The cavalry companies fighting to the last in sternest
    heroism,
In the midst of their little circle, with their slaughter'd
    horses for breastworks,
The fall of Custer and all his officers and men.

Continues yet the old, old legend of our race,
The loftiest of life upheld by death,
The ancient banner perfectly maintain'd,
O lesson opportune, O how I welcome thee !

As sitting in dark days,
Lone, sulky, through the time's thick murk looking in
    vain for light, for hope,

From unsuspected parts a fierce and momentary proof,
(The sun there at the centre though conceal'd,
Electric life forever at the centre,)
Breaks forth a lightning flash.

Thou of the tawny flowing hair in battle,
I erewhile saw, with crest head, pressing ever in front,
    bearing a bright sword in thy hand,
Now ending well in death the splendid fever of thy deeds,
(I bring no dirge for it or thee, I bring a glad triumphal
    sonnet,)
Desperate and glorious, aye in defeat most desperate,
    most glorious,
After thy many battles in which never yielding up a gun
    or color,
Leaving behind thee a memory sweet to soldiers,
Thou yieldest up thyself.

                                        Walt Whitman

From emujscerm gouer ... and slumbery froze,
The sun that in the rosy clouds con ele,
Beam in the ... softer,
Broad for the life g...

Thou of the town's throng help in ...
Revealing ... thy head, pressing my ... in fair,
Bearing a bright sword in thy hand ...
New smiling with a laugh ... would her with ...
I ... the might ... the As ... Thing ...

Desperate and of ... in ... in delair and ...

the ... wo her ... wish the plain ...

Notes.

NOTES.

BRYANT, WILLIAM CULLEN.—American. Born 1794; died 1878. Bryant's genius is not seen to best advantage in his "Wild-Life" poems. It is in meditation verse, such as the "Thanatōpsis" and "Lines to a Water-fowl," that the majesty and grave eloquence which characterise his genius become most readily apparent.

CHENEY, JOHN VANCE.—American. Born 1848. Author of *Thistle Drift*, a volume of wayward and captivating lyrics, and of some of the strongest magazine verse of the day. Mr. Cheney is public librarian at San Francisco.

DUVAR, JOHN HUNTER.—Canadian. Born 1830. Lives in Prince Edward Island. Retired Lieutenant-Colonel of the Canadian Militia. In 1879 he published "The Enamorado," a closet drama of the Spanish school; and in 1888 a volume containing "De Roberval"—a Canadian drama; and other poems. In turn of thought, and in diction, Colonel Duvar's work displays a strong tinge of mediævalism. There is an admirable song-quality in his briefer lyrics.

EATON, THE REV. ARTHUR WENTWORTH.—Canadian. A
Church of England clergyman. Born in Nova Scotia.
Now living in New York. Author of *The Heart of
the Creeds*, a view of historical religion in the light
of modern thought, published in New York in 1888.

FAWCETT, EDGAR.—American. Poet and Novelist. Born
1847. Lives in New York, and is a close student of
New York life, of which his admirably-wrought novels
form the best transcript to be had. Mr. Fawcett's
poetry is of exquisite finish and strong intellectuality.
His diction is remarkably rich.

GILDER, RICHARD WATSON.—American. Poet and Editor.
Born 1844. Editor of the *Century Magazine*. Author
of "The New Day," "The Poet and his Master,"
"Lyrics," "The Celestial Passion." Mr. Gilder has
given us some of the most impressive sonnet-work of
the period, sincere, and filled with a sort of reverent
rapture.

GUINEY, LOUISE IMOGEN.—American. Born 1861. Lives
in Boston. Author of "Songs at the Start," "Goose-
quill Papers," "The White Sail," and other poems.
Miss Guiney's work is of very unusual promise, showing
marked vigour and originality, held well in hand by an
exacting *technique*.

HAMILTON, IAN.—Scottish. Lieutenant-Colonel Hamilton,
born 1854, is the author of the well-known *Jaunt
in a Junk*, and of a romance of singular promise

entitled *Icarus.* The poem by which he is represented in this anthology is from his charming little volume, *The Ballad of Hadji, and other Poems.*—(Kegan Paul & Co., 1888.)

HORNE, RICHARD HENGIST.—English. Born 1803; died 1884. Author of "Gregory VII.," "Cosmo de Medici," "Ballads and Romances," "Orion," etc. His masterpiece, "Orion," is a great poem, characterised by a severe majesty and an admirable breadth of effect.

DE KAY, CHARLES.—American. Born 1849. Lives in New York. Author of "Hesperus," "The Vision of Nimrod," "The Vision of Esther." Mr. De Kay's verse is essentially large in conception and in treatment. Often faulty in detail, through impatience rather than through lack of technical skill, this poet's work possesses a passionate strength and an affluent magnificence which are peculiarly to be valued in these days of dilettantism. His "Wild-Life" verse gives little idea of his powers.

LANIER, SIDNEY.—American. Born 1842, in Georgia ; died 1881, in Baltimore, where he held the position of Lecturer in English Literature in John Hopkins' University. Author of *Poems, The Science of English Verse, The English Novel and its Development,* etc. It is difficult for the friends of Lanier to speak temperately of his genius, which has not yet won the general homage that is unquestionably its due. Lanier's death was a loss to American literature, relatively almost equal to that which England sustained in the death of Keats. With a matchless gift of cadence, intensest humanity and sincerity, rich creative imagination, and intellectual powers of the highest order, he was advancing, I believe, to the chief place in American song, when death stayed him. As it is, he will always be among poets a stimulating force.

MACHAR, AGNES MAULE.—Canadian. Lives in Kingston, Ontario. Author of many fugitive poems in American and Canadian periodicals. Miss Machar has a firm command of musical and simple lyric forms, and of vivid description. She writes usually under the *nom-de-plume* of "Fidelis."

MACINTYRE, DUNCAN BAN.—This foremost of modern Gaelic poets was born in the Strath of Glenorchy on 20th March 1724. His compositions are still universally popular in the Scottish Highlands (west and north-west), and are characterised by remarkable fire and poetic beauty. Duncan Ban Macintyre died in 1812.

MAIR, CHARLES.—Canadian. Born 1840. Has spent much of his life in the Canadian North-west, with the history of which his name is intimately associated. Author of *Dreamland, and other Poems,* and "Tecumseh," a drama. This latter work, a highly-imaginative and forceful dramatic study, fresh in treatment and faithfully Canadian in tone, has given Mr. Mair perhaps the foremost position among Canadian poets.

MACKAY, ROBERT.—This popular Gaelic poet was born in the Strathmore of Sutherlandshire, about the year 1714, and died in 1778.

MILLER, JOAQUIN.—American. Born 1841. Real name, Cincinnatus Hiner Miller. The nick-name of Joaquin, which he accepted gracefully when just past boyhood, was given him in remembrance of a noted Mexican bandit, whom he had the ill-fortune to resemble, and in whose stead he came near being hanged. Fervidly sensuous, vividly pictorial, utterly frank, with a rich imagination fed on familiarity with the most gorgeous life and landscapes earth can afford, Mr. Miller is easily first among the singers of wild life. Author of *Songs of the Sierras ; Songs of the Sun Lands ; The Ship in the Desert ; The Danites ; Songs of the Mexican Seas,* etc., etc.

O'REILLY, JOHN BOYLE.—American. Born in Ireland, 1844. Editor of the *Boston Pilot.* Author of *Songs, Legends, and Ballads ; Moondyne,* and *The Statues in the Block, and other Poems.* He has had an exciting career, having been in political exile in Western Australia, whence he made his escape to America. His verse is masculine, spontaneous, and novel.

POCOCK, H. R. A.—A young Englishman in the Canadian North-west. He has done some picturesque verse, but little that comes within the scope of this collection.

PRINGLE, THOMAS.—Scottish. Born 1789 ; died 1834. He spent a part of his life in Cape Colony, and, on his return, wrote a volume called *African Sketches,* prose interspersed with verse. This work contains the well-known and stirring lines which I have quoted in the text.

ROBERTS, CHARLES GEORGE DOUGLAS.—Canadian. Born 1860, in New Brunswick.

SANGSTER, CHARLES.—Canadian. Born 1822. Lives in Kingston, Ontario. Author of *The St. Lawrence and the Saguenay, and other Poems;* and *Hesperus, and other Poems and Lyrics.* Honoured as the pioneer among distinctively Canadian poets.

SHARP, WILLIAM.—Scottish. Born 1856. Mr. William Sharp's " Wild-Life " verse, the fruit of a sojourn in the wilds of Gippsland and New South Wales, and of a voyage in the Pacific, is characterised by that direct and interpretative truthfulness which constitutes the enduring charm of his *Transcripts from Nature.* In its feeling for the romantic and the supernatural, Mr. Sharp's song has a special significance.

STEDMAN, EDMUND CLARENCE.—American. Poet, and leader of American literary criticism. Born 1833. Author of " Alice of Monmouth," " The Blameless Prince," " The Lord's Day Gale," and other poems ; and of those masterpieces of creative and inspiring

criticism, the *Victorian Poets* and *Poets of America*.
Mr. Stedman's verse is spontaneous, untrammelled by
dogmatic theory, and ranges from the passionate
abandon of "The World Well Lost," the virile fire
of "Osawatomie Brown," to the delicate humour of
"The Doorstep."

STODDARD, RICHARD HENRY.—American. Poet and critic.
Born 1825. Lives in New York. Author of "The
King's Bell," "The Book of the East," etc. I know of
no other English-speaking poet of the day who can
turn a song so gracefully and easily as Mr. Stoddard
can. Certain of his lyrics are, to my mind, unsur-
passed for haunting charm of cadence. He has also
written several odes of admirable nobility and
stateliness.

TEGNER, ESAIAS.—Swedish. Born 1782; died 1846. Bishop
of Wexiö. Translation by Professor Stephens, of the
University of Copenhagen.

THOMPSON, MAURICE.—American. Born 1844. Lives at
Crawfordsville, Indiana. Author of "Songs of Fair
Weather," "The Witchery of Archery," "A Talla-
hassen Girl," etc. Mr. Thompson's verse is of the
finest which America is now producing. It displays
a wholesome delight in life, an exquisite out-door
purity, and a resonant baritone quality, such as one
associates with the note of a hunter's horn.

WARNER, HORACE EVERETT.—American. Born 1839. Lives in Washington. Has published no volume. His writings in prose and verse appear in various American magazines. The poem quoted is a version of a Dakotah legend.

WHITMAN, WALT.—American. Born 1819. Lives in Camden, New Jersey. Author of *Leaves of Grass*, the title now given to his collected poems. Whitman is a force in modern poetry. He has sought to give new and striking expression to what is distinctive in American life, by breaking with the accepted laws of poetic form. With his profound humanity, his breadth, strength, and insight, I believe that he has proved himself a great poet,—but this in spite of, and not by means of, his contempt of form.

Printed by WALTER SCOTT, *Felling, Newcastle-on-Tyne.*

www.ingramcontent.com/pod-product-compliance
Lightning Source LLC
Chambersburg PA
CBHW031423020726

47499CB00005B/1568